Lattegan's Loot

Lucky Larry Lattegan, the famed and feared outlaw, is languishing in Cougar Creek jail, waiting to be hanged. But rumour on the outside has it that his ill-gotten gains lie buried somewhere in the rough and impenetrable terrain of the Medicine Bow Mountains.

Among those eager to discover the exact location of the treasure are Marshal Matt Gruber, the voluptuous bar singer Belle Nightingale, the unscrupulous saloon-keeper Bart Kingston with his hired guns, and two of Lattegan's old gang. It would be a bitter battle when they all clashed.

Gruber is thankful to have with him his old friend, the Kentuckian gunfighter Jack Stone, for when the chips are down there's no one deadlier than Stone.

Lattegan's Loot

J.D. KINCAID

A Black Horse Western

ROBERT HALE · LONDON

© J.D. Kincaid 2001
First published in Great Britain 2001

ISBN 0 7090 6916 2

Robert Hale Limited
Clerkenwell House
Clerkenwell Green
London EC1R 0HT

Photoset by
Derek Doyle & Associates, Liverpool.
Printed and bound in Great Britain by
Antony Rowe Limited, Wiltshire.

ONE

Lucky Larry Lattegan was due to celebrate his fortieth birthday on Midsummer Day, 21 June 1879. Not that this was much cause for celebration, for Lattegan's famous luck had seemingly run out. He was currently languishing in a cell at the rear of Cougar Creek's law office, where he awaited execution by hanging. By an unlucky chance, this was scheduled for the very morning of his birthday.

Outside Lattegan's cell it was a baking-hot afternoon, the sun scorching down out of an azure-blue Wyoming sky upon the small cattle town. The date was 18 June and the town council had gathered in the bar-room of the Cougar Creek Hotel. There were six members altogether. They sat round a large rectangular table, which was situated in the centre of the room directly beneath a slowly revolving fan. This fan had little effect, however. It merely rotated the hot, stale air.

5

Hiram G. Culpepper mopped his brow with a large, red-silk handkerchief. He was a short, rotund man dressed in a city-style grey suit and sporting a large black beaver hat. Bright blue eyes twinkled as he twirled his walrus moustache and gazed round the table. He had about him a preening, self-important air and he addressed his fellow-councillors in a loud, fruity voice.

'In my capacity as mayor, I have brought you all here today to discuss the forthcomin' hangin' in our town,' he stated pompously.

'What's there to discuss?' demanded Warren Gilchrist, manager of the Cattlemen's Bank across the street, a tall, lean, dyspeptic-looking individual with thinning peppery hair and a long nose, on the bridge of which was balanced a pair of pince-nez.

'I wondered that when you asked to use this room for our meetin',' commented Mrs Annie Rogers, the rosy-cheeked, buxom widow who owned the Cougar Creek Hotel.

'Me, too,' said Fred Hope, a large, jolly-faced man, and one of the two storekeepers present.

The other, Lou Anderson, small and ferrety, nodded sagely and added, 'We all got businesses to run, Hiram. We cain't jest be up an' leavin' 'em at the drop of a hat.'

'You have employees,' retorted the mayor.

'Even so. I spend 'nough time attendin' the

regular council meetin's without you goin' an' callin' an additional one,' snapped Anderson.

'Yeah. I mean, what's this hangin' to us?' enquired Hope.

'It could be extremely profitable, for it's gonna attract folks from all over the county, indeed from all over the state,' declared Culpepper.

'Maybe even from other states,' opined Dan Mason, coming in on the mayor's side.

Hiram G. Culpepper smiled gratefully at the lawyer, a tall, imposing figure, with lofty, aristocratic features, who was elegantly attired in an immaculate three-piece beige suit and white, low-crowned Stetson.

'Exactly,' said the mayor.

'So, what's the problem?' demanded Annie Rogers.

'The problem,' said Culpepper, 'is that not all the folks the hangin's likely to attract will be entirely desirable. The hands from the Lazy S for example.'

'Hell, they ride in most Saturdays!' exclaimed Fred Hope.

'An' git drunk an' cause trouble.'

'Not that much trouble, Hiram,' said Lou Anderson.

'Only 'cause the sheriff an' his deppity see to it that they don't.'

'So?' said Annie Rogers.

7

'So, Annie, my dear, Jim Blake an' young Tom Jeffers are gonna have more'n jest those danged cowboys to tend to,' declared Culpepper.

'The mayor's right,' said Dan Mason. 'We don't know what kind of riff-raff this hanging will bring into town.'

'Aw, I figure you two are bein' a mite alarmist!' cried Annie.

'Would you say that Sheriff Jim Blake is an alarmist?' enquired Culpepper.

'No, I wouldn't say so,' replied the widow.

'Wa'al, he wants to recruit four extra deppities for the period up to an' includin' the day of the hangin'.'

'Four extra deputies!' exclaimed Warren Gilchrist in astonishment, his pince-nez flying off his nose as he spoke.

'That'll cost the town a packet!' remarked Fred Hope.

'Which is why I called this meetin', Fred,' explained the mayor. 'In order to discuss the sheriff's request.'

'Mebbe you did right to call it after all,' admitted Lou Anderson, and then, lighting up a cigar, he drawled, 'Surely we ain't expectin' that big an influx of folks?'

'Some have arrived already,' said Culpepper. 'Indeed, a few have booked into this here hotel. Ain't that correct, Annie?'

The widow inclined her head.

'I guess so, Hiram.'

'Wa'al, there could be many more arrivals tomorrow an' the day after. An', among the medicine-men, fortune-tellers, card-sharps, jugglers an' assorted mountebanks who are sure to hit town, there's bound to be several cutpurses an' pickpockets.'

'Not to mention those desperadoes, who didn't quite see eye to eye with Lattegan and are intent on watching the sonofabitch swing,' added the lawyer.

'That's right, Dan,' said Culpepper. 'An', of course, it's always possible some of his old gang might try to spring him.'

'You think so?' exclaimed Annie in alarm.

'I dunno, Annie. But I sure as hell wouldn't wanta bet agin' it,' declared the mayor.

'So, are you saying, Hiram, that Sheriff Blake is justified in requesting that we appoint and pay for four extra deputies?' enquired Gilchrist.

'I reckon I am,' said Culpepper.

'Surely two would be more than sufficient?' said the banker.

'Jim Blake don't think so,' retorted Culpepper.

'Yeah, wa'al, the wages ain't comin' outa his pocket,' snapped Lou Anderson.

'You want yore store smashed up an' yore goods stolen, do yuh?' said Culpepper.

'Hell, no!' cried the storekeeper.

'Wa'al, that could happen,' said Culpepper. 'Sheriff Blake an' Deppity Jeffers are surely gonna have their work cut out these next few days keepin' law an' order.'

'Which is why Jim Blake has requested four extra deputies. Of course, if you don't mind a massive increase in crime and disorder . . .' began Dan Mason.

'I ain't sayin' that!' protested the storekeeper.

'And we don't know that such will be the case,' asserted Gilchrist.

'No?' The lawyer eyed the banker coldly and asked, 'Are you prepared to take that chance?'

'I don't believe we can afford to,' stated Culpepper. 'It's our duty as councillors to put the safety of our citizens an' the integrity of our town before anythin' else.'

'Fine words!' sneered Gilchrist.

'Which'll cost us dear if 'n' we do as you suggest,' added Fred Hope glumly.

'What do you say, Annie?' asked Culpepper.

'I've listened to all the arguments an' I honestly don't know whether or not we shall need those additional peace officers. 'Deed, none of us can know for certain one way or the other,' said the widow.

'So?'

'So, Hiram, I figure we gotta trust the sheriff's

judgement. Fred said it'll cost us dear if we recruit the deppities. Wa'al, it could cost us a great deal more if we don't an' Jim Blake's proved right.'

The two storekeepers, Fred Hope and Lou Anderson, mulled this over, as did the banker, Warren Gilchrist. They did not look entirely convinced, yet the widow's words had provided them with food for thought.

Culpepper waited a few moments, hoping that Annie Rogers' remarks would have the desired effect.

'OK,' he said finally, 'unless anyone's got anythin' further to say on the subject, I suggest we vote.'

'Yeah, let's do that,' averred Anderson.

The others nodded their agreement, whereupon Culpepper smiled and then stated, 'The question is this: Do we support our sheriff by allocatin' sufficient funds to pay for the four extra deppities he reckons he'll need?'

'Up to and including the day of the hanging, but no longer,' interjected Warren Gilchrist.

'Exactly, Warren,' replied the mayor. 'All those in favour?'

He immediately raised his hand, as did Dan Mason and Annie Rogers. Slowly, and somewhat reluctantly, Lou Anderson and Fred Hope followed suit. All eyes turned upon the banker, Warren Gilchrist. He sighed heavily.

'Guess I'd better make it unanimous,' he said finally, and he, too, raised his hand.

'Excellent!' exclaimed the mayor. 'I'll go tell Jim Blake.'

'That's it, is it?' enquired Annie Rogers.

'Yes, unless anyone's got anythin' else they'd like to raise?' said Culpepper. The others shook their heads. 'OK, then, I declare that this here extraordinary council meetin' is now concluded,' he stated.

And so it was that, a few minutes later, the mayor crossed to the south side of Main Street and entered the law-office, which was situated plumb in the centre of the town. It consisted of a large front office and, at its rear, a narrow passage and five cells. At the present time, only the middle one of the five was occupied, and that, of course, housed the man whose forthcoming hanging the town council had been discussing, Lucky Larry Lattegan.

Culpepper found both the sheriff and his deputy busy poring over a batch of Wanted notices.

Sheriff Jim Blake was a tall, lean man in his early forties, with grizzled grey hair, faded blue eyes, a narrow face and a lantern jaw. He wore a check shirt, Levis and a brown leather vest on to which was pinned his badge of office. He carried a Colt Peacemaker tied down on his right thigh, and his grey Stetson hung on a peg on the wall immediately behind him.

His deputy, Tom Jeffers, was barely twenty years old, of average height, but powerfully built and dressed similarly to the sheriff, except that his vest and his Stetson were black. Cheerful, enthusiastic and fresh-faced, the youth, too, carried a Colt Peacemaker in his holster.

'Howdy, Jim, Tom,' Culpepper greeted the two lawmen.

'Afternoon, Hiram. How'd it go? What was the council's verdict?' asked Sheriff Jim Blake, coming straight to the point.

'It was unanimous,' replied the mayor. 'You git yore four deppities up to an' includin' the day of the hangin', jest like you asked for.'

'I knew I could rely on you to swing it,' said Blake, with a broad grin, for he was well aware of Culpepper's susceptibility to flattery.

'Yes, wa'al, I s'pose I did present a darned good case,' replied the mayor.

''Course you did,' declared Blake.

'I don't want nothin' to go wrong. This town's likely to do real good business over the next three days, an' I'm relyin' upon you to keep law 'n' order on the streets.'

'Tom an' I'll do our best. Won't we, Tom?'

'Sure will, Sheriff,' replied the young deputy eagerly.

'An' those additional deppities'll help,' said Blake. 'I'll go deputize 'em this very afternoon.'

'You got some fellers in mind?' enquired Culpepper curiously.

'Some of our youngsters. Luke Barnard, the blacksmith's son, for one. I want 'em young an' tough,' explained the sheriff.

'Good! I'll leave it to you then, Jim, I got several businesses to run.'

This was no more than the truth, for Hiram G. Culpepper owned the livery stables, leased out several commercial premises, had a share in two of the town's three saloons and an interest in the stockyards. As well as being mayor, he was Cougar Creek's richest and most influential citizen.

When Culpepper had departed, shutting the door behind him, Jim Blake lit a cheroot and sighed heavily.

'You ain't none too happy 'bout this whole danged thing, are yuh, Sheriff?' said Tom Jeffers.

Blake viewed the young deputy with a gloomy eye.

'No, I ain't,' he muttered. 'I can smell trouble comin',' he added sourly.

He recalled only too clearly that day, three months earlier, when Lucky Larry Lattegan and his gang had ridden into Cougar Creek. Mid-March, and with a biting wind blasting in from

the plains and through the town; it had been
bitterly cold. He closed his eyes and conjured up
the scene, as bright and vivid as though it were
only yesterday.

There were five of them altogether. They rode
into town in their brown derby hats and long,
ankle-length brown leather coats. The leader was
tall and lean, with a hawkish, pockmarked face
and drooping black moustache. His eyes were cold
and black as pebbles. Lucky Larry Lattegan was
an unscrupulous desperado who, during the
course of his career, had committed a whole string
of murders and robberies.

His four companions were of the same breed.
Vince Cody was heavily bearded and built like an
ox, Abe Gutman small and shifty-eyed, Joe
Flaherty squat, scar-faced and with lank, shoulder-length hair and a wispy goatee, while Mad
Dog Mel was bearded like Cody, but considerably
smaller, though with as grim and ugly a visage as
one was ever likely to encounter throughout the
length and breadth of the West.

Main Street was deserted that wintry afternoon when they rode in from the east. With any
luck at all, the gang would have reached the
Cattlemen's Bank quite unobserved. But that was
the day Lucky Larry Lattegan's luck deserted
him, for Nat Sheridan, editor and proprietor of
the Cougar Creek *Gazette*, happened to glance out

of his office window just as they were riding past. And he straightway recognized Lattegan and Mad Dog Mel.

A few years earlier, when working as a reporter in Abilene, he had covered the trial of both men for a stagecoach robbery. They had been acquitted through lack of evidence and the brilliance of their defence lawyer. Nat Sheridan, however, had remained convinced of their guilt. Their arrival in town was not, he decided, good news.

Consequently, he had headed straight for the law-office and alerted Sheriff Jim Blake. By a quirk of fate, he had found the office full of armed men, twelve in all, for Blake was in the process of forming a posse to ride out in pursuit of a band of renegade Indians. Blake determined that that could wait until after they had tackled Lattegan and his gang.

'C'mon, men,' he rasped, 'let's go git them sonsofbitches!'

Abe Gutman, whom Lattegan had left outside the Cattlemen's Bank as look-out, promptly discharged his Remington revolver upon spotting the sheriff and his companions. They, for their part, had drawn their weapons and were rushing headlong down the street towards the bank.

They arrived within shooting range just as Lattegan and his other three companions, alerted by Gutman's shot, dashed out of the bank.

Immediately, Blake cried halt, but the outlaws ignored this order, so he and his party straightway opened fire. The result was that both Abe Gutman and Vince Cody were shot dead, Gutman having his brains blown out and Cody receiving no fewer than six .45 calibre slugs in his chest.

The outlaws returned fire, but hastily, as they attempted to mount their horses. Only one of Blake's men was hit and he merely suffered a minor flesh wound to the upper arm. Nevertheless, this response gave the outlaws a little breathing space, sufficient for all three survivors to clamber into their saddles. They promptly wheeled their horses round and set off in the direction from which they had come, away from the sheriff and his posse.

'They're gittin' away!' cried Blake.

A fusillade followed the bank-robbers down Main Street. Joe Flaherty and Mad Dog Mel were already out of range of the townsfolk's sixguns, but Lucky Larry Lattegan was not. His roan was shot from under him and he hit the street with a tremendous thud. This knocked the wind out of him and, by the time he had recovered his senses, he found Jim Blake, Tom Jeffers and the rest standing over him and pointing their revolvers at him. His Colt Peacemaker lay on the ground a couple of feet away, but he made no attempt to reclaim it.

'Got you, yuh murderin' bastard!' snarled the sheriff.

'Yeah, but will yuh hold me?' retorted Lattegan.

'Oh, we'll hold you OK! An' we'll hang you,' said Jim Blake, with a grin.

'That's right. Yo're gonna swing, Mr Lattegan,' promised Tom Jeffers.

That had been then. Now, three months later, Lucky Larry Lattegan had been tried and found guilty on several counts of murder and robbery. His hanging was scheduled to take place in three days' time, on Midsummer Day. It had been a long-winded process. Sheriff Jim Blake was glad that it was nearly at an end.

'I jest hope an' pray that everythin' goes accordin' to plan,' he said fervently.

'Why shouldn't it, Sheriff?' enquired Tom Jeffers.

'No real reason. It's simply a feelin' of forebodin' that I got.'

'You think that even at this late date some of his ol' pals might try to spring him?'

'Wa'al, Joe Flaherty an' Mad Dog Mel ain't never been caught. An' there are others who rode with Lattegan at different times. They might be tempted to try.'

'Tempted?'

'Yes, Tom. Tempted by Lattegan's loot.'

'You b'lieve that story 'bout Lattegan buryin'

his share of the gang's hauls somewheres in the mountains hereabouts?'

'I dunno. But some of his confederates might. An', if 'n' he did, wa'al, there could be a tidy amount buried. After all, he participated in one helluva lotta robberies over the years, an', as leader of the gang, I guess he took the lion's share each time.'

'So, what are yuh sayin', Sheriff?'

'I'm sayin', Tom, that we gotta keep our eyes peeled till Lattegan's good an' hanged.'

Jim Blake smiled grimly. Then he rose and went across to the door that led from the office to the rear quarters. He pushed it open and stepped into the narrow passage beyond, on one side of which stood five cells. He stared at the occupant of the middle cell.

Lucky Larry Lattegan sat on a narrow wooden bench beneath a small, barred window that looked out on to the plains to the south of the town. He was attired in a white cambric shirt, black trousers and black boots. His brown leather coat, beige jacket and brown derby hat lay in a heap at the far end of the bench.

'Come to check I'm still here?' he sneered.

Blake stared into the outlaw's coal-black eyes and smiled.

'Wa'al, I surely ain't here for the pleasure of lookin' at yore ugly mug,' he replied. 'Jest wanted to know if yo're needin' anythin'?'

'I'm clean outa cheroots,' stated Lattegan

'I'll git yuh some,' promised the sheriff. He grinned and added, 'I ain't the kinda feller to deny a man who'll soon be dancin' at the end of a rope.'

TWO

US Marshal Matt Gruber stared stonily at the snake. He had dismounted to attend to his horse, which had seemingly gone lame. The cause was easily detected: a small stone lodged in the roan's left hind hoof. Gruber was in the process of removing this stone when he spotted the rattler.

He had inadvertently disturbed the rattler and, alarmed and angry, the snake had reared up ready to strike. The snake's ominous rattle had alerted the lawman to his danger, but too late. There was no way he could reach for, draw and fire his revolver before the rattlesnake struck.

The venomous reptile thrust forward its head with lightning speed, its fangs bared. Gruber flinched and involuntarily closed his eyes. As he did so, a shot rang out and the rattler's head was blasted from its body. Gruber's eyes opened wide and he stared open-mouthed at the headless body of the snake, its tail thrashing about in the death-throes. He glanced across at the horseman who had ridden up and who was returning his Frontier Model Colt to its holster.

'Jack! Jack Stone!' he exclaimed.

'Howdy, Matt,' replied the horseman, with a grin.

The two men were old friends whose paths had crossed several times in the past in the days when Jack Stone, too, was wearing a badge and doing his level best to uphold law and order.

Matt Gruber studied the man who had just saved his life. What he saw was a tall, broad-shouldered Kentuckian, six-foot two-inches in his stocking-feet and consisting of nigh on 200 pounds of muscle and bone. Stone's thirty-odd years had left their scars, both physical and mental. The bullet-wounds had healed, but the broken nose remained and the emotional wounds, which made Stone the man he was, would never fully heal. His square-cut features had been handsome once and, even now, when he smiled, he regained something of his former good looks.

The Kentuckian wore a red kerchief round his strong, thick neck. A grey Stetson, grey shirt, faded denim pants and unspurred boots, and a knee-length buckskin jacket completed his apparel, while tied down on his right thigh was the Frontier Model Colt. And he rode a bay geld-ing.

Stone returned the other's gaze. Matt Gruber was looking older than the Kentuckian remem-bered him. The marshal's jet-black hair was now tinged with grey, his moustache completely grey. But he was as slim and upright-looking as ever, a dapper figure in a low-crowned black Stetson, black Prince Albert coat, trousers and boots, a light grey vest and black bootlace tie. He, too, carried a revolver tied down on his right thigh, but his was a Colt Peacemaker. His dark, satur-nine features split into a broad smile as he reached up and shook Stone's hand.

'What are yuh doin' up in these parts, Jack?' enquired Gruber.

'Jest finished drivin' cattle up the Goodnight-Lovin' trail from San Antonio to Cheyenne,' replied the Kentuckian.

'Yeah?'

'Yeah. So, I figured I'd relax for a while. Mebbe go off an' do a li'l huntin'. They say there's good sport to be had up in the mountains of the Laramie range. That's where I'm headed.'

'Wa'al, it's lucky for me you happened along, else that goddam rattler would've done for me.'

'You don't survive that varmint's bite.'

'You sure as hell don't!'

'So, what're you doin' these days, Matt? Still

workin' outa the US marshals' office in Laramie?'

'Yup. I'm on my way to the small cattle-town of Cougar Creek. Chief Marshal John Downie wants me to interview Lucky Larry Lattegan. You remember Lattegan, don't yuh, Jack?'

''Course I do. Road-agent, bank-robber, a stinkin', lousy, cold-blooded killer who hangin's too good for.'

'Wa'al, hangin's what he's gonna git.'

'You don't say!'

'I do, Jack. The sonofabitch tried to hold up the bank in Cougar Creek a few months back, an' got hisself caught. He's been tried an' convicted an' is scheduled to swing on Midsummer Day.'

'It's the eighteenth today, ain't it?'

'That's right. I expect to reach Cougar Creek 'bout midday. That'll give me three days before they hang him.'

'To do what, Matt?'

'To persuade Lattegan to tell me where he's hidden his loot.'

'That's yore assignment?'

'It is. Y'see, a good portion of Lattegan's ill-gotten gains is US Government money, wages intended for Fort Brandon, which he an' his gang stole from the pay-wagon. They bushwhacked the detail, killin' three an' woundin' five of the soldiers.'

'An' you figure you can git Lattegan to divulge

what he's done with the money?'

'I can try.'

'I wish you luck, Matt, but what makes yuh think he's hid his share of that or any other robbery?'

'Rumour has it that he has. Some place up in the mountains.'

'Which mountains?'

'The Medicine Bow range.'

'D'yuh b'lieve this rumour?'

'I dunno, Jack. Mostly his kind spend their money on women an' whiskey an' gamblin'. But Lattegan, he's a pretty shrewd operator. It's jest possible he could've buried his loot somewhere, intendin', when he has accumulated what he considers to be enough, to dig it up an' use it to provide himself with a life of ease in 'Frisco, say, or in one of the big cities on the Eastern seaboard.'

'I s'pose.'

'Anyways, when I reach Cougar Creek, I aim to go interview Lucky Larry Lattegan.'

'An' if he won't talk?'

'I'll keep tryin'.'

'Up until they take him out an' hang him?'

'Yup. There ain't no law says I can only interview the sonofabitch once.'

'I guess not.'

'Why don't you ride along with me, Jack?' enquired Gruber. 'Rest up in Cougar Creek for a

few days 'fore you go off huntin', mebbe stay an'
see the hangin'?'

'Wa'al. . . .'

'I'd appreciate yore company, Jack.'

'But yo're gonna be kinda busy, Matt.'

'I won't be interviewin' Lattegan mornin', noon
an' night.'

'No?'

'Hell, no! A few hours each day, that's all. Until
he talks.'

'If he talks.'

Stone noted that Gruber, although determined
to do his duty, did not sound particularly opti-
mistic. He surmised that Gruber considered Chief
Marshal John Downie had sent him on something
of a wild-goose chase.

'OK,' said Stone, 'I guess I'll hang around a few
days an' keep yuh company. But I probably won't
wait to watch the hangin'.'

'No?'

'No, Matt. I ain't overly fond of 'tendin'
hangin's.'

'Fair enough.' Matt Gruber smiled. The
Kentuckian's company would be very welcome
during the period leading up to the execution of
the outlaw. 'Jest stop over for as long as you feel
inclined,' he said.

The two men rode on through the morning.
Both were hot and dusty by the time they reached

26

Cougar Creek. The town consisted of only the one street: Main Street; and they cantered along this thoroughfare until they found the law-office.

'Wa'al, Jack,' said Gruber, pulling up his roan, 'I figure on droppin' in here, for I'm told Lattegan is incarcerated in a cell at the rear of this office.'

'Fine; I'll see yuh later.' Stone pointed towards the Cougar Creek Hotel a little further along Main Street. 'I'm gonna book myself a room in that there hotel,' he said. 'We can meet up there when you've concluded yore interview.'

'See you then, Jack.'

Matt Gruber promptly dismounted, hitched his horse to the rail outside the law-office and went inside. Jack Stone, meanwhile, rode on past the hotel to the livery stables, where he left the gelding with instructions that it should be curried, fed and rested.

He then made his way back along the sidewalk to the Cougar Creek Hotel, arriving there just as the noonday stage disgorged some of its passengers on to the stoop outside. The first to step down was a young woman, veiled and in widow's weeds. Stone courteously offered her his arm and helped her to alight.

At this point, Annie Rogers and her porter emerged from the hotel. The hotelier enquired who, if any, of those who had alighted from the stage, required a room. Upon finding that only the young woman in black intended to patronize her establishment, she instructed the porter to take care of the young woman's luggage while she escorted her into the hotel.

Jack Stone followed Annie and the woman in black through the hotel entrance and down a narrow lobby to a desk at the foot of the stairs that led to the upper floor. Here balding, bespectacled Benny Brooks, the hotel clerk and receptionist, presided. Benny Brooks turned the register on his desk so that it faced the new guest and, with a flourish, produced a pen.

'Later, Benny,' said Annie. 'Firstly, I shall show Mrs . . . er. . . ?'

'Lattegan,' replied the woman in black.

Annie started, but quickly recovered her aplomb.

'I . . . I shall show Mrs Lattegan upstairs.' Annie smiled at her guest. 'There is a choice of rooms, Mrs Lattegan, and I should like you to have the one you'll feel most comfortable in,' she explained silkily.

'Thank you,' said the woman in black.

The two women thereupon headed upstairs, followed by the porter carrying the newcomer's luggage.

Stone watched them ascend the stairs. As far as he knew, he had never met or seen Lattegan's wife, yet the young woman seemed vaguely familiar. He turned to the clerk.

'I, too, would like a room. An' a certain Matt Gruber will likely book in a li'l later. He has some business to attend to first,' said the Kentuckian.

'OK! If you'll jest sign here.'

Stone promptly obliged.

'That do?' he asked.

'Yeah. I'll . . . er . . . I'll show yuh to yore room, Mr Stone,' said the clerk.

Stone grinned and followed Benny Brooks upstairs. It was evident that his name was not known to the clerk. This suited Stone fine and dandy, for his days as a lawman, deputy in Dodge City to Bat Masterson and the man who tamed Mallory, had earned him a reputation that he was keen should be forgotten. Nowadays, he tried, as far as possible, to avoid trouble.

The room assigned to him, while sparsely furnished, was both clean and tidy and overlooked Main Street.

'Will this suit, Mr Stone?' enquired Benny Brooks.

'Yup. It'll do jest fine,' said Stone. 'But, tell me, what are the chances of me gittin' a bath, for I'm kinda hot 'n' dusty?'

'I'll have one drawn for you immediately, sir,' promised the clerk.

Benny Brooks was as good as his word. And so it was that Jack Stone was wallowing in hot, soapy water, and puffing contentedly on a cheroot, when the young woman in black eventually emerged from the room she had chosen and made her way downstairs. Benny Brooks was back in position and, this time, he succeeded in getting her to sign the register.

'Tell me,' she said, once she had completed this small task, 'in which direction does the jail lie?'

'We ain't exactly got a jail,' said Brooks. 'Only a few cells back of the law-office.'

'Would my husband be occupyin' one of those cells?' she enquired.

'Yes, ma'am; I reckon he would,' replied the clerk.

'Then kindly point me in the direction of the law-office,' said the woman.

Benny Brooks accompanied her out onto the stoop and promptly gave her the necessary directions.

Thus it was that, a few minutes later, the woman dropped in on Sheriff Jim Blake and his deputy.

'Afternoon, Sheriff,' she said.

'Afternoon, ma'am,' replied Blake, peering up at the black-clad figure, whose face was concealed behind her veil. 'How can I help you?' he asked.

'I've come to see my husband,' said the woman.

'Yore husband?'

'Larry Lattegan.'

30

'Yo're his wife?'

'I am.'

'Yo're dressed up like yo're already his widow,' commented the sheriff.

'Yeah, an' he ain't dead yet,' added Tom Jeffers.

'No; but he soon will be. Today's the eighteenth an' he's due to swing on the twenty-first,' stated the young woman.

'True,' admitted Blake.

'So, I figured I'd dress up accordin'ly 'fore I set out.'

'You come far?'

'Yes, Sheriff, from Wichita in the State of Kansas.'

'The news sure has spread!'

'It certainly has. Anyway, can I go see Larry?'

'I'm afraid not, Mrs Lattegan. Not straight away. You'll have to come back.'

'Why, Sheriff?'

' 'Cause there's a US marshal in there with him at the moment.'

'An' why would a US marshal wanta speak to Larry?'

'That ain't for me to say, Mrs Lattegan.'

'No?'

'Nope. So, if 'n' you'll give it an hour or so an' then come back, I'm pretty sure the marshal will have finished an' you'll be able to see yore husband.'

The woman sighed heavily.

'OK,' she said. 'I'll return later.'

'Good-day, then, Mrs Lattegan.'

'So long, Sheriff.'

Leaving Sheriff Jim Blake and his deputy to their duties, the woman headed back towards the hotel. Since she had plenty of time to kill, she dawdled along the sidewalk, pausing and peering into the windows of the various shops and stores. Consequently, a good half-hour or more had elapsed between her leaving and returning to the Cougar Creek Hotel.

As she entered its portals, she almost collided with Jack Stone, who, having had his bath, was on his way to the hotel bar-room.

'Sorry, Mrs Lattegan,' he muttered.

'You are in a hurry, Mr . . . er. . . ?

'Stone, Jack Stone. Yes, I've got me one helluva thirst an' I'm kinda anxious to slake it.' The Kentuckian grinned and asked, 'You care to join me, ma'am?'

The woman inclined her head.

'Why not?' she murmured and preceded Stone into the bar-room.

The bar-room of the Cougar Creek Hotel was pretty plush by Wyoming standards. It boasted a superb gleaming mahogany bar counter, tables and chairs from the same expensive wood, several settees and couches padded and covered in red velvet, and a magnificent mirror running the full length of the bar counter and beautifully engraved.

At that hour of the afternoon, however, the bar-room was practically deserted. Stone and the young woman strolled across to the bar.

'What'll you have?' enquired the Kentuckian.

'A large red-eye,' replied his companion. 'You can bring it over to that there corner table.'

Stone frowned. He had not expected the girl to ask for that. And still he felt there was something vaguely familiar about her. Yet he could not say exactly what it was. He turned to the bartender and ordered a beer for himself and a large whiskey for the young woman.

'OK,' he said, as he planted the glass of whiskey down on the table in front of her. 'Guess if yo're aimin' to drink that there whiskey, you'll have to lift that veil.'

'You lift it, Jack.'

Stone stared hard at the woman. The voice. He recognized it. He stretched out his hand, took hold of the veil and threw it back.

'Goddam it, it's Belle! Belle Nightingale!' he exclaimed.

'Hi, Jack, how're yuh doin'?' enquired the woman, smiling seductively at him.

Belle Nightingale was a blonde in her late thir-ties, a little worn round the edges and rather more buxom than when in her prime, yet still remarkably attractive. She had, in her time, been a sporting woman and a saloon singer in various cattle towns across the West. In consequence, her path and Stone's had crossed on several occasions. Indeed, more than once he had sampled her ample charms. Dodge City and Abilene sprang to mind.

'What was all that "You are in a hurry, Mr . . . er . . ." nonsense?' Stone demanded.

'Jest joshin', Jack.'

'You recognized me from the start?'

'Sure did.'

'I see. So, tell me, when the hell did yuh marry Lucky Larry Lattegan?'

'Wa'al, I didn't exactly marry him.'

'Whaddya mean? You've been passin' yoreself off as Mrs Lattegan ever since you hit town.'

'We was lovers once.'

'So?'

'For over a year.'

'What are yuh sayin'?'

'I'm sayin' he might easily have married me.'

'An' that gives you the right to call yoreself Mrs Lattegan?'

'I guess.'

'But why'd yuh wanta, Belle?'

'Because, Jack, the sheriff ain't gonna let me in to see him as jest plain ol' Belle Nightingale.'

'You ain't plain an' you ain't old.'

34

'You know what I mean. The sheriff cain't deny the right of the wife of a condemned man to visit him.'

'I s'pose not. But why in tarnation do yuh wanta visit him?'

'You've heard the rumour, surely?'

'What rumour?' Stone guessed that Belle was referring to the story that US Marshal Matt Gruber had told him earlier. He decided to play dumb, however, and said again, 'What goddam rumour?'

'The rumour that Larry has buried his share of all them bank robberies an' stagecoach hold-ups he an' his gang have perpetrated somewhere up in the mountains north of here.'

'Do you honestly believe that, Belle?'

'I sure do. I got to know Larry pretty darned well an', I'm tellin' yuh, he was one helluva devious feller. In fact, it would surprise me if he *hadn't* salted away his loot.'

'OK, you could be right. But how, in blue blazes, d'yuh reckon yo're gonna persuade Lattegan to divulge its location?'

'I'll use my feminine charms.'

Stone laughed.

'You sayin' I ain't got no feminine charms?' demanded Belle irately.

'Nope. Yo're a mighty attractive woman. But it's gonna need more 'n' jest charm to make Lucky

Larry Lattegan spill the beans.'

'We was as near as dammit man an' wife for over a year! Surely that must mean somethin' to Larry?'

'Wa'al. . . .'

'That loot ain't gonna be no good to him when he's hanged.'

'True, Belle.'

'So, I figure he may as well tell me where it's hidden.'

'Mebbe. Anyways, I wish you luck, Belle.'

'Thanks, Jack.' The blonde glanced anxiously at the Kentuckian and murmured, 'You won't tell nobody that I ain't Larry's wife, will yuh?'

Jack Stone consulted his conscience. Should he tell his old friend, Matt Gruber? Or perhaps the sheriff? Since he considered that Belle's chances of eliciting the whereabouts of Lattegan's loot were almost certainly nil, he saw no reason to betray her secret.

'No, Belle,' he promised, 'I won't tell a soul that you ain't Lucky Larry Lattegan's ever-lovin' spouse. You got my word on that.'

'Gee, thanks, Jack!' Belle cried, and impulsively she leant across the table, intending to kiss him.

'Hold fire,' grinned Stone. 'You wanta git folks talkin'?'

'Oh, hell, no!' she replied, and promptly sank back in her chair.

'You want folks to b'lieve yo're Mrs Lattegan, yo're gonna have to play the part,' remarked Stone.

'Yeah, yo're right, Jack. Thanks again.' Belle took a large gulp of her whiskey. 'That sure ain't gonna be none too easy,' she confessed, with a sassy smile.

THREE

On that same afternoon, the Hot Spot Saloon in Laramie was doing rather more business than the bar-room in the Cougar Creek Hotel, but then it was the busiest and the best of the town's four saloons. Two bartenders were being kept reasonably busy, the roulette wheel was surrounded by a small crowd of gamblers and games of poker, blackjack and faro were all in progress.

Presiding over all this was the saloon's proprietor, Bart Kingston, a short, fat man with a smug, self-satisfied smirk on his pale, podgy face. His black city-style suit and derby hat were both of the finest materials, while a sparkling white shirt showed above the crimson-brocade vest which stretched tightly over his stout little belly. A neat black tie and highly polished black leather shoes completed the picture. Bart Kingston did not, like most of his customers, carry a handgun on his thigh, but instead sported a long-barrelled .30 calibre Colt in a shoulder-rig beneath the black jacket.

His smile slipped as he observed the two strangers push their way in through the batwing doors. Although they had drastically changed their appearance since he had seen them last, he at once recognized Joe Flaherty and Mad Dog Mel. Flaherty had had his once shoulder-length hair shorn so that it was nowhere longer than one inch, and he had shaved off the wispy goatee. Mad Dog Mel had similarly had his hair cut short and removed the heavy beard. Both had exchanged their long, ankle-length brown leather coats and derby hats for check shirts, brown leather vests, blue denim pants and grey Stetsons. Bart Kingston noted that, as of old, they carried hand-guns, Joe Flaherty a Remington and Mad Dog Mel a Colt Peacemaker.

Kingston glanced round anxiously and caught the eye of the Cobb brothers. Jake and Gil Cobb were big, rawboned men, with harsh, tough-looking visages. They dressed entirely in black and each carried a pair of Army Colt revolvers. They were employed by Kingston to protect his premises, to deal with any unruly customers and ensure that nobody, a drunken cowboy or a disgruntled gambler perhaps, smashed up the saloon. Their treatment of all troublemakers was fast, efficient and invariably brutal.

The two brothers left their respective positions and loped across the bar-room to join their employer.

'Somethin' the matter, boss?' growled Jake Cobb.

'I hope not, but I want you fellers at my back jest in case,' replied Bart Kingston.

'In case of what?' enquired Gil Cobb.

'In case I git any trouble from them two.' Kingston nodded towards the outlaws who, by this time, were leaning against the bar-counter and ordering beers. 'Joe Flaherty an' Mad Dog Mel,' he muttered in an undertone.

Jake Cobb whistled.

'Hell, they rode with Lattegan, didn't they?' he asked.

'Sure did. They were with Lucky Larry when he got hisself captured,' replied the saloonkeeper.

'That was in Cougar Creek. No more'n ten miles from here,' stated Gil Cobb.

'That's right. An' his hangin's scheduled for Midsummer Day, three days from now,' said Kingston.

'You figure they're on their way there, aimin' to attend the hangin'?' enquired Cobb.

'Mebbe.'

'But surely that'd be takin' one helluva risk? They could be recognized an' then . . .'

'They've changed their appearance considerably. You'd have to know 'em pretty darned well to recognize 'em.'

'An' you do, boss?' said Gil Cobb.

'I knew 'em in the old days. Back in Dodge City. That was some hell-town 'fore Masterson an' Stone cleaned it up.' Bart Kingston smiled thinly. 'I'm gonna mosey over an' have a quiet word with 'em. Jest be ready to back me up if 'n' the sonsofbitches try anythin',' he remarked.

'Will do, boss,' said Jake Cobb.

'Yup. We'll be right behind you,' added his brother.

Kingston nodded and thereupon strolled slowly across to the bar, where he confronted the two newcomers.

'Howdy, boys; ain't seen you in a while,' he said cheerfully.

The outlaws turned to face him. Their faces were deadpan and there was not the slightest glint of recognition in the eyes of either man.

'Do we know you?' growled Mad Dog Mel.

''Course you do. Bart Kingston, proprietor of this here establishment, at yore service,' said Kingston, adding quietly, 'More to the point, I know both of you.'

'You could be mistaken,' hissed Mad Dog Mel.

'I don't think so,' said Kingston.

'Wa'al, jest in case you are, don't go bandyin'

our names around,' said Joe Flaherty in a voice loaded with venom.

'Wasn't gonna,' replied the saloonkeeper. 'Jest stepped over to buy you boys a drink for old times' sake.'

Mad Dog Mel finished his beer at one draught and plonked the empty glass on the counter.

'Thanks,' he said. 'Same again.'

'An' me,' added Joe Flaherty, swiftly draining his glass and standing it next to his companion's.

'You boys aimin' to stay long here in Laramie?' enquired Kingston, offering the two desperadoes cigars while the bartender replenished their glasses.

'What's it to you?' grunted Mad Dog Mel.

'Nothin' at all,' said Kingston. 'Jest wondered whether I'd be havin' the pleasure of yore company in the Hot Spot for a while?'

'Wa'al, you won't,' stated Flaherty firmly.

'No?'

'Nope. We're jest passin' through. Ain't that so, Mad Dog?'

'Sure is,' agreed the other.

'On yore way to watch the hangin'?'

'What goddam hangin'?' snarled Mad Dog Mel.

'The hangin' of yore one-time associate, Lucky Larry Lattegan. It's due to take place not ten miles from here, at the small cattle-town of Cougar Creek.'

'Is that so?' said Flaherty.

'Rumour has it that you two fellers were with him when he got hisself caught,' remarked Kingston.

'I hope you ain't intendin' to spread that rumour,' growled Mad Dog Mel, 'for me an' Joe, we wouldn't take it none too kindly if 'n' you did.'

'We sure wouldn't!' exclaimed Flaherty.

'I . . . I wouldn't dream of it,' protested the saloonkeeper. He took a long pull at his cigar before continuing, 'So, if you ain't plannin' to go see Lattegan's hangin', jest what are yuh doin' in these parts, huh?'

'What's it to you?' rasped Mad Dog Mel, repeating his earlier question.

'I'm simply curious, that's all,' said Kingston.

'You'd best remember, Mr Kingston, that curiosity killed the cat,' said the outlaw.

'But, as it happens, it ain't no big secret,' interposed Flaherty genially.

'No?'

'Nope. We dropped in to Laramie to enjoy a coupla beers an' pick up some supplies. Then, we're headin' on north. Aimin' to have us a spot of relaxation: a li'l huntin' an' fishin'.'

'Ah! Wa'al, I sure hope you both have a pleasant trip.' Bart Kingston took another puff at his cigar and then remarked, 'You'll have to excuse me, boys, for I got some paper work to catch up on. So, in case I don't see you when you leave, I'll say goodbye.'

'So long,' replied Joe Flaherty, while Mad Dog Mel merely grunted.

Leaving the two outlaws to their cigars and beers, Bart Kingston turned and headed alongside the bar-counter towards the door that opened into his office. The Cobb brothers followed. Kingston placed his hand on the door handle, then paused and, speaking in a low voice, said:

'Jake, keep yore eye on them two critters an' let me know immediately they leave the saloon. Gil, while Jake's fetchin' me, you follow 'em outside an' observe exactly where they make for. OK?'

'Sure, boss,' the brothers chorused.

Bart Kingston retired to his office. He had in fact no paper work to attend to, but simply sat behind his desk, smoking and thinking. It was possible that the outlaws had purchased their supplies before entering the Hot Spot Saloon. However, he suspected not. Hot and dusty and straight off the trail, they would surely have wanted to quench their thirst with some ice-cold beer prior to chasing up supplies?

It was also possible that they did intend heading north and enjoying a little sport. But again he suspected not. The fact that they were back within ten miles of the scene of their ill-fated bank raid, and this within a few days of the date fixed for Lucky Larry Lattegan's hanging, was just too much of a coincidence. Kingston was convinced that they were up to something, and he was determined to find out what it was.

In the event, he hadn't been in his office half an hour when Jake Cobb knocked on the door and, without waiting for a response, burst in.

'Boss, they've finished their beers an' up an' left!' he cried.

'Thanks, Jake.'

Bart Kingston rose and followed the hired gun out of the office. They hurried across to the batwing doors. Gil Cobb stood outside on the stoop. There were several people going about their business in Main Street, but of Joe Flaherty and Mad Dog Mel there was no sign.

'Where the hell did those two go?' demanded the saloonkeeper.

'Over there,' replied Gil Cobb, pointing across the street towards Phil Campbell's general store. 'They're still in there,' he added.

'OK. Thanks, Gil. You an' Jake can go back inside.'

Bart Kingston dropped into the rocking-chair which he kept outside the saloon. When business was slack, he liked to sit outside on the stoop and watch the world go by. He leant back, lit a fresh cigar and waited.

Ten minutes later the outlaws emerged from

the store. Whatever it was they had purchased, it was wrapped in brown paper and Joe Flaherty was carrying it. They stepped down into the street to where their horses were hitched. Flaherty placed the brown paper package with great care into one of his saddle-bags, then they mounted their horses. They set off northwards.

Bart Kingston reflected that there was good hunting and fishing to be had in the mountain country to the north of Laramie. So, Joe Flaherty could have been telling the truth. On the other hand, Cougar Creek lay approximately ten miles to the north.

Once the desperadoes had disappeared beyond the town limits, Bart Kingston rose and waddled slowly across the street. He clambered up on to the opposite sidewalk and entered Phil Campbell's general store. Once inside, the saloon keeper made his way past various piles of merchandise towards the counter, where Phil Campbell, an elderly, white-haired fellow in a dark-green apron, was giving instructions to his assistant. The storekeeper completed these as Bart Kingston approached.

'Afternoon, Bart, what can I do for you?' he enquired.

'You've jest had a coupla strangers in,' said Kingston.

'Yeah. That's so.'

'I'd like you to tell me what they purchased.'

Phil Campbell stared curiously at the saloon-keeper.

'Why would yuh wanta know that?' he asked.

'That's my business, Phil. Are you gonna tell me?' Kingston retorted.

'Guess there ain't no harm in tellin' you. They purchased a pair of wire-framed spectacles.'

'A pair of spectacles!'

'Yeah. It was kinda strange. The uglier one of the two, he pushed the lenses out an' then put 'em on. I ask yuh, what in tarnation's the point of wearin' specs without lenses?'

Bart Kingston smiled sourly. Mad Dog Mel was evidently not entirely happy with his change of appearance and was hoping the spectacles would complete the transformation.

'Is that all they bought?' he demanded.

'Hell no! They also bought half a dozen sticks of dynamite, the same number of fulminate caps an' a length of continuous fuse.'

'Jeeze!'

'Said they were goin' prospectin' for gold.'

'An' you believed them?'

'I didn't have no reason to disbelieve 'em.'

'No, I guess not. OK, thanks, Phil.'

'You ain't buyin' nothin'?'

'Not today.'

Bart Kingston retraced his steps to the Hot

Spot Saloon. The information he had gleaned from Phil Campbell had given him much food for thought. His suspicions, he felt, had been well founded. Joe Flaherty and Mad Dog Mel were heading for Cougar Creek. He was pretty darned sure of that.

On his return to the saloon, he beckoned the Cobb brothers into his office.

'Shut the door, boys, an' sit down,' he said amiably, as he dropped into his chair behind the desk.

'Them two fellers leave town?' enquired Jake Cobb.

'Yeah.' Kingston grinned broadly and asked, 'Guess what they purchased off Phil Campbell.'

'Search me,' said Jake Cobb.

His brother merely scratched his head.

'Dynamite,' said Kingston.

'Holy cow!'

'Told Phil they was goin' prospectin' for gold.'

'That wasn't what they told you, boss,' remarked Gil Cobb.

'No.'

'So, whaddya think they're up to?'

'I think they are plannin' to visit Cougar Creek an' spring Lucky Larry Lattegan from jail. But not outa loyalty.'

'No?'

'No, Gil. You must've heard the story 'bout

Lattegan buryin' his loot someplace up in the mountains of the Medicine Bow range.'

'An old wives' tale,' growled Jake Cobb.

'I thought that once,' said Kingston. 'But I ain't so sure now. As you said earlier, Jake, they'll be takin' one helluva risk headin' back to Cougar Creek, for, make no mistake, they were with Lattegan when he raided the bank there.'

'You reckon?'

'I reckon. An', despite their changed appearance, there's always a possibility they'll be spotted. So, they've gotta have a mighty powerful reason to take that risk. Wa'al, I figure it's gotta be Lattegan's loot that's lured 'em back. They want a share of it.'

'Lattegan's been pretty goddam successful over the years,' remarked Jake Cobb. 'He could, I s'pose, have a fortune stashed away.'

'Exactly,' said Kingston.

'You reckon Joe Flaherty an' Mad Dog Mel are plannin' to blast Lattegan out that jail?' enquired Gil Cobb.

'I do,' affirmed the saloonkeeper. 'Why else would they have purchased dynamite?'

'How much?'

'Half a dozen sticks.'

'Hmm. That's a lot more'n they'll need to blow a hole in jest the one wall. If 'n' they ain't careful, they could blow up the entire jail an' Lattegan with it!' exclaimed Jake Cobb.

'Yeah. I hope they know what they're doin',' sighed Kingston.

'What's it to you, boss?'

'I aim to be there an' grab me a share of Lattegan's loot,' stated the saloonkeeper.

'Wa'al, I'll be hog-tied!' cried Gil Cobb.

'I intend settin' out straight away for Cougar Creek.' Bart Kingston smiled amiably at the two brothers. 'An' I want you boys to ride with me,' he added.

The brothers looked surprised.

'But, boss,' said Jake Cobb, 'if we all three ride out, who's gonna look after the Hot Spot?'

'Baldy will cope. I don't expect we'll be gone more'n a few days,' replied Kingston.

The saloonkeeper was, in truth, none too happy at the prospect of leaving his saloon to the care of Baldy Harris, the older of his two bartenders, but the lure of Lattegan's fabled loot was more than he could resist. It was a chance he had to take, or he would regret not taking it for the rest of his life.

The brothers exchanged glances.

'OK,' said Jake Cobb, 'we'll ride along.'

'But we'll want even shares,' remarked Gil Cobb.

Bart Kingston shrugged his shoulders. He didn't know exactly what to expect when he reached Cougar Creek. However, he realized that, to have any chance of sharing in Lattegan's ill-gotten gains, he would need the support of his two hired guns.

'Agreed,' he said and, rising from his chair, he stretched out his hand towards the brothers.

The deal was settled with a handshake.

FOUR

Some miles to the south of Laramie stood the Arapaho Indian reservation. Chief Mighty Bear had signed a treaty with the white men and now he and his tribe were confined to a barren and unyielding patch of land. It was imprisonment in all but name.

Mighty Bear's tribe, like all other Plains Indian tribes confined to reservations, was at the mercy of an Indian agent, a white man appointed by the US Government to administer the funds and provisions necessary for the Arapahos' survival. Rex Curtis, in common with many of his kind, had no love for the Indians and happily lined his own pocket by cheating and robbing them of their dues. Mighty Bear had complained to Colonel Walter K. Benson, the commander of nearby Fort Raeburn, but to no effect. The Colonel had no more love for the Indians than had the agent and dismissed the chief's complaints out of hand.

In consequence of the privations suffered and the callous treatment meted out to them, several of Mighty Bear's young bucks had attempted to flee the reservation. Six had been captured and brought back alive, seven had been brought back dead. The latest to abscond, a nineteen-year-old named Wolf That Sings, remained at large. He had broken out three days earlier, leaving behind his younger brother, Wolf That Speaks, and their two close friends, Spotted Tail and Little Elk.

The sun beat down out of a cloudless blue sky as Spotted Tail made his way from his tepee towards the Indian agent's trading post. Spotted Tail, a tall, lean figure with flashing black eyes, high cheek bones and a hawklike visage, was attired in buckskins and wore three eagle's feathers in his head-dress. He carried no firearm, but had a hunting-knife in an embroidered sheath at his waist. And he was no less discontented than those of his fellows who had fled the reservation. Conscious that his chief's protests to Colonel Benson had proved fruitless, Spotted Tail determined to have matters out with the Indian agent. However, realizing that Mighty Bear would probably forbid him from tackling the agent, the young brave had told nobody of his intention.

Spotted Tail approached the trading post on

silent, moccasin-clad feet. The front door was wide open and he entered without knocking. Piles of boxes and crates containing provisions stood between the doorway and the rear of the store, where Rex Curtis was entertaining a visitor. Although he could not see them, Spotted Tail could hear what they were saying, for, like most of the younger generation of Arapahos, he had been taught the white man's tongue. Mighty Bear had insisted upon this, stating that the Indians' future was almost certain to be controlled by their white conquerors and, therefore, their very survival could well depend upon their understanding the white man's language.

Spotted Tail slowly wended his way between the stacks of provisions towards the sound of the two men's voices.

Rex Curtis, fat and florid with slicked-back black hair and walrus moustache, stood leaning against the store counter, while his visitor, a lanky, thin-faced fellow in a grey city-style three-piece suit and derby hat, sat on a tall stool. Between them, planted on the counter, was a large, capacious carpet-bag, from which the visitor had produced several bottles of whiskey. His name was Nat Spooner and he was a whiskey salesman.

The two men had been drinking steadily for an hour or more, Spooner hoping to persuade the Indian agent to purchase a supply from the stock he carried aboard his covered wagon, which was standing outside.

'Where are yuh aimin' for after here?' Curtis was asking the whiskey salesman as the Arapaho approached the counter.

'Wa'al, I'd hoped to make it to Cougar Creek in time for the hangin',' said Nat Spooner. 'There'll be a fair crowd there, an' I figure I'd've made me a pretty profit. Only I won't git there in time. On horseback, yes; but on that ol' wagon of mine, nope.'

'What hangin'?' enquired Rex Curtis curiously.

'The hangin' of Lucky Larry Lattegan,' replied Spooner.

'Ain't he hanged yet? He was took a long time back,' said Curtis.

'I know, but the law, it cain't be hurried.'

'S'pose not.'

'It's a darned shame 'bout the loot.'

'What loot?'

'Lattegan's loot. You must've heard the story: how, over the years, he's hidden most of his booty somewheres up in the mountains.'

'Yeah. You b'lieve that ol' story?'

'I do. An' there it's likely to remain. As I jest said, it's a darned shame.'

'Unless Lattegan reveals its whereabouts 'fore he hangs.'

'To who? Not to the sonsofbitches who're gonna string him up, that's for sure.'

'No.' Curtis smiled grimly. Then, as Spotted Tail emerged from amongst the stacks of merchandise, he growled, 'Whaddya want, redskin?'

'The corn that you owe my people,' replied the Indian.

'What goddam corn? You've had yore ration. You got what you paid for,' retorted Curtis.

'No. There were several bushels short.'

'Who says?'

'I say.'

'An' who the hell are you, but a stinkin', lousy red savage!' Curtis straightened up and, stretching behind him, lifted a bull-whip from its peg on the wall. 'You dare to accuse me of cheatin' yore people! Wa'al, I'm gonna teach you to keep yore lyin' mouth shut in future,' he snarled.

'That's it, Mr Curtis! You tell him, an' you whip him real good!' cried Nat Spooner.

'I intend to,' stated the Indian agent, his eyes gleaming wickedly.

He rounded the counter, the bull-whip coiled and ready. He drew it back, but, before he could lash out, Spotted Tail acted. The Arapaho drew and threw the hunting-knife in one lightning-fast movement. The blade was out of its sheath, through the air and deep into Rex Curtis's chest in a split second. Such was the force exerted by Spotted Tail, the knife went in right up to the hilt.

Curtis screamed, dropped the whip and

grabbed at the hilt. Before he could begin to with-draw the blade, however, Spotted Tail leapt upon him and, knocking aside his hand, grasped the knife and ripped upwards with all his might, lift-ing the agent bodily with the razor-sharp blade. Curtis screamed a second time and then fell back and collapsed on to the floor. His eyes glazed over and he was dead even before Spotted Tail could retrieve the knife from his chest.

Nat Spooner, meantime, sat transfixed on the tall stool. A combination of too much whiskey, and the shock of seeing the Indian agent so swiftly and ruthlessly cut down, had cast him into a kind of stupor. Belatedly, he stirred and attempted to pull out the double-barrelled Derringer that he kept hidden up his right sleeve. But he was too late. The Derringer was only half-way out when Spotted Tail plunged the already bloodied blade deep into his belly. Spooner toppled backwards off the stool and hit the floor with a thud. He groaned once, then lay there, staring sightlessly at the ceiling, while Spotted Tail once more retrieved his hunting-knife. The Arapaho cleaned the blade on the whiskey salesman's jacket and then replaced it in its sheath.

Realizing that the die was now cast, Spotted Tail hurried from the trading post and headed back towards the tepees. He found his friends, Little Elk, a slim, smiling eighteen-year-old, and

Wolf That Speaks, a stocky, stone-faced youth of the same age, sitting outside Little Elk's tepee.

'You ... you have blood on you!' exclaimed Little Elk.

'Yes.'

'What ... what have you done?' asked Wolf That Speaks in alarm.

'I went to speak to Curtis, but he would not listen.'

'He has never listened to Mighty Bear. Why would he listen to you?' enquired Little Elk.

'I told you, he did not.'

'No.'

'What happened?' said Wolf That Speaks.

'He tried to whip me. So I killed him,' replied Spotted Tail.

'You ... you will have to flee!' cried Little Elk.

'Yes. We have talked of it often. Now the time for talking is past.' Spotted Tail turned to Wolf That Speaks and said, 'I shall follow in your brother's footsteps. I shall have my freedom again.'

'Where will you go?' asked Wolf That Speaks.

'North. Across the border into Canada. I shall be safe there, and I am told there is good hunting.'

'Canada is a long way from here.'

'Yes, Wolf That Speaks. Will you come with me? And you, Little Elk?'

Spotted Tail's two friends glanced at each other. Finally, Little Elk spoke.

'I will come, Spotted Tail,' he said. 'I, too, desperately want my freedom, and here, on the reservation, that I do not have.'

'Wolf That Speaks?' said Spotted Tail.

'Yes. I should have gone with my brother. Perhaps we shall meet. He spoke of heading for Canada.'

Spotted Tail smiled.

'Canada is a big country,' he said. 'But, if we are to go, we must go now before the white men find out that Curtis is dead. Therefore, say your farewells quickly and meet me at the trading post. I shall go and tell Mighty Bear that we intend leaving the reservation.'

The three friends hurriedly took their leave of their families; Spotted Tail explained to his chief the need for his sudden departure and then all three donned buffalo robes, saddled their horses and, having placed their rifles in their saddle-boots, mounted and trotted off in the direction of the trading post, where they were to rendezvous.

On arrival there, Spotted Tail dismounted and went inside. A few moments later, he emerged bearing several small boxes of ammunition and three Remington revolvers. He shared out the ammunition and gave Little Elk and Wolf That Speaks each a revolver. Then he remounted and the three Arapahos set off northwards away from the reservation.

They rode steadily for the remainder of the morning and well into the afternoon. The sun was just beginning to set in the west when they found themselves entering a narrow gulch with high, precipitous walls on both sides. They had progressed about half a mile into it when, rounding the bend ahead of them, there appeared a small party of riders.

The Arapahos slowed their pace, their hearts thumping wildly as they recognized the horsemen to be bluecoated soldiers of the US Cavalry. There were three of them: Sergeant Bill McDowd and Troopers Henry Larsen and Pete Evert.

Bill McDowd was a thick-set, craggy-faced veteran, whose contempt for all civilians was equalled only by his hatred of the redskins. His two companions were both lean, gawky youngsters, Larsen blond and Evert dark-haired, who, under McDowd's tutelage, had, during their three years' service, built up a hatred of the Indians almost equal to his own. These three, when sent out from Fort Raeburn to apprehend a runaway Arapaho, invariably brought him back dead.

On this occasion, Colonel Benson had sent them off in pursuit of Wolf That Speaks' brother, whom they had eventually tracked down and cornered in a box canyon several miles north of the Wyoming–Montana border. His dead body was draped across, and tied to, the back of a small spindle-shanked cayuse. The sight of his brother's corpse caused Wolf That Speaks to cry out.

'Wolf That Sings!' he screamed. 'You . . . you have killed him.'

Sergeant Bill McDowd grinned viciously.

'Goddam right, we have!' he snarled. 'That red sonofabitch didn't know when he was well off.'

'And when was that?' enquired Spotted Tail.

'When he was livin' on the reservation,' replied McDowd.

'Living! You call that living?' exclaimed Spotted Tail.

'It's the best you goddam savages can expect,' said the sergeant.

'Is that so?' said Little Elk.

'Yeah, it is so,' responded O'Dowd. 'Which prompts me to ask, what in tarnation are you three doin' out here?'

'We are seeking our freedom,' declared Spotted Tail.

'Hear that, boys?' sneered McDowd. 'These stinkin' redskins are seekin' their freedom.'

'That makes 'em runaways,' drawled Larsen.

'Renegades,' said Evert.

'Sure does,' agreed McDowd.

The three bluecoats grinned.

'I guess it's our duty to arrest 'em,' remarked Larsen.

61

'That's right, boys,' said McDowd. 'We're bound to take 'em in.'

As he spoke, the sergeant's hand dropped on to the butt of his Army Colt, while the two troopers made a grab for their carbines. Taking the Indians in dead was clearly their intention. But they had reckoned on the Arapahos carrying only the rifles that rested in their saddle-boots. They were in for a rude awakening.

All three Arapahos threw open their buffalo robes and whipped out the Remingtons that they had earlier stuck in their belts. Spotted Tail was the first to fire.

His shot struck Bill McDowd in the chest and knocked him backwards out of the saddle. Little Elk, meantime, drilled a neat hole in the centre of Henry Larsen's forehead and Wolf That Speaks pumped a slug into Pete Evert's belly.

Larsen was dead before he hit the ground, while Evert, dropping his carbine and grasping at his belly, was subsequently struck by a volley of shots, three from Little Elk and two from Wolf That Speaks. Blood spurted forth from a variety of wounds and he too was dead by the time he hit the ground.

Only Sergeant Bill McDowd remained alive.

The sergeant had lost possession of his revolver and struggled to sit up. As he did so, Spotted Tail leapt from the saddle and ran up to him. The

Arapaho rammed the muzzle of his Remington hard against McDowd's skull, between his eyes.

'You die, paleface murderer!' hissed Spotted Tail.

'N . . . no! Goddammit, you surely wouldn't kill a man in cold blood!' exclaimed the sergeant.

'My blood is not cold. It is hot, heated by my hatred for you, white man,' retorted Spotted Tail and, without more ado, he squeezed the trigger and blasted the sergeant's brains out through the back of his skull.

Spotted Tail smiled grimly. Then, ramming the still-smoking Remington into his belt, he bent over the dead soldier and carefully removed a pair of binoculars, which McDowd had draped over one shoulder.

'Why do you take those, the white man's glasses?' enquired Wolf That Speaks.

'You can see for many miles through them,' explained Spotted Tail. 'Which could be useful when we go hunting.'

'That is true,' said Wolf That Speaks.

'And also if we are hunted,' added Spotted Tail, whereupon he climbed back into the saddle and the three Arapahos resumed their journey north-wards.

FIVE

US Marshal Matt Gruber was not a happy man. His interview with Lucky Larry Lattegan had been less than satisfactory. The bank robber had refused categorically to divulge the whereabouts of his loot. Indeed, he had declared that the story, that he had hidden a large proportion of his ill-gotten gains somewhere in the mountains of the Medicine Bow range, was simply that, a story. Gruber didn't believe the outlaw, but had been unable to shake him. He would, of course, try again. It was his duty to do so, yet he feared that Lattegan would remain silent and take his secret with him to the grave.

Gruber's return to the Cougar Creek Hotel was observed by Belle Nightingale from her bedroom window. Her room, like Stone's, overlooked Main Street. She noted the marshal's grim visage and smiled to herself. He did not look like a man who had tasted success. She guessed that he was probably in need of a good, stiff drink and was headed for the hotel bar-room, which she and Jack Stone had only lately vacated. She waited a few minutes, therefore, to give the lawman time to settle himself at the bar. Then she left her room and hurried downstairs.

At the reception desk, Belle handed her key to the clerk, Benny Brooks, and then proceeded in stately fashion along the narrow hallway and out into Main Street. Once outside, she turned to her right and set off in the direction of the law-office.

The office was situated only a few minutes' walk away. When she reached it the blonde found Sheriff Jim Blake on his own.

'Howdy, Sheriff,' she said. 'I'm back.'

'So I observe, Mrs Lattegan,' replied Blake.

'You gonna let me see my husband this time?' enquired Belle.

'I guess so.'

'That US marshal finished his business with Larry?'

'He has.'

'Good!'

Jim Blake took Belle Nightingale through into the rear of the law-office, where the five cells were located. Only the centre cell was occupied. Belle raised her veil as she confronted its occupant.

'You got a visitor,' said Blake to his prisoner.

Lucky Larry Lattegan smiled thinly.

'So it would seem,' he drawled.

'I'll leave you to it, then,' said Blake.

Neither Belle nor Lattegan spoke, not until the sheriff had returned to the outer office and closed the connecting door behind him. Then, confident that they were unlikely to be overheard, Lattegan broke the silence.

'What's the idea of the widow's weeds, Belle?' he enquired.

Belle laughed.

'I'm wearin' 'em in anticipation of yore hangin',' she replied.

'But you ain't my wife.'

'The sheriff don't know that.'

'You surely ain't callin' yoreself Mrs Lattegan?'

'But I am, Larry.'

'Why in tarnation would you do that?'

'If 'n' I hadn't, the sheriff sure as hell wouldn't've permitted me to talk to you.'

'I s'pose not.' Lattegan eyed the woman quizzically and demanded, 'But, then, why d'yuh wanta talk to me?'

'We were lovers once.'

'So?'

'So, mebbe I wanta talk to you for old times' sake.'

'An' mebbe I'm the President of these here United States!'

'Aw, c'mon, Larry!'

'No, you come on, Belle. You ain't here to ask after my health.'

'Not much point, with you 'bout to be hanged.'

'So, why are you here? Last I heard you was in Wichita. That's one helluva long ways from Cougar Creek.'

'Yeah.'

'Wa'al. . . ?'

'OK, I'll tell you straight.'

'Go on.'

'That loot you buried up in the Medicine Bow mountains, it ain't gonna be no good to you when yo're dead.'

'So?'

'So, hows about tellin' me where it's hid?'

Lucky Larry Lattegan laughed harshly.

'Why the hell would I wanta do that?' he rasped.

'For old times' sake,' suggested Belle sweetly.

'For old times' sake? Yo're pretty darned fond of usin' that phrase.'

'Wa'al, why not? Like I said, we were lovers once an' . . .'

'You ran out on me.'

'I wouldn't put it quite like that.'

'No?'

'No, Larry. I left you for . . .'

'A goddam piano-player.'

'I was gonna say, I left you for the very good reason that you refused to give up yore life of crime. I got sick of forever bein' on the run. I jest wanted to settle down.'

'With yore piano-player?'

'With someone. Anyone. The piano-player wasn't disposed to stay put though. He had itchy feet an' kept movin' on. After a while, we split up.'

'So, have you settled down since, Belle?'

The blonde smiled wryly.

'Nope. Not yet,' she confessed. 'You were right about me bein' in Wichita. I was employed there as a singer in Lou Jardine's saloon.'

'That's new, Belle. I never knew you could sing.'

'It beats workin' as a sportin' woman. Pays better, for one thing.'

'I guess it does at that.'

'Wa'al, hows about it, Larry? Are you gonna tell me where you got all that loot stashed?'

Lucky Larry Lattegan shook his head.

'Nope. If 'n' I do hang, I aim to take that li'l secret with me to the grave.'

'Whaddya mean, if 'n' yuh do hang? They're buildin' the scaffold as we speak.' Belle glanced across the cell. Through the barred window, workmen could be seen erecting the platform on which Lattegan was due to be executed. 'The date's set for Midsummer Day,' she stated bluntly.

'My birthday,' remarked Lattegan.

'Gee, that's kinda unfortunate!' exclaimed Belle.

'Aw, it don't matter much what day they hang me!' retorted the outlaw.

'*If* they hang you. You said, *if* they hang you.'

'That's right, Belle. Where there's life, there's hope.' Lattegan grinned and added quietly, 'A feller would sure be grateful to anyone who sprung him.'

'Now, wait a minute, Larry!' cried the blonde.

'Jest think about it, Belle. You git me outa here an' I'll share the loot with you. You let me hang, then you ain't never gonna lay yore hands on it.'

'But how in blue blazes am I supposed to spring you? I'm a saloon singer for Pete's sake, not some gun-totin' desperado!'

'That's up to you, Belle. You want a share of that loot, you'd best find a way.'

Belle opened her mouth to protest further, then thought better of it.

'OK,' she said. 'I'll think about it. But don't go gittin' yore hopes up, Larry,' she warned the outlaw.

'I won't,' replied Lattegan.

'Be seein' yuh, then.'

''Bye, Belle.'

The blonde returned to the outer office, where she was greeted by Sheriff Jim Blake.

'You leavin', then, Mrs Lattegan?' he enquired.

'That's right, Sheriff, though I may pop in again, mebbe tomorrow or the day after, if that's all right with you?' said Belle.

'That's fine by me,' said Blake.

'Thank you, Sheriff.'

Belle smiled at the lawman, then left the office and stepped outside into the late afternoon sunshine.

Belle Nightingale dined alone that evening in the dining-room of the Cougar Creek Hotel. Jack Stone and US Marshal Matt Gruber sat together at a separate table. Belle noted that Stone studiously avoided looking in her direction. She assumed, therefore, that the Kentuckian intended to keep his promise not to betray her secret to his friend, the marshal.

'I'm wastin' my goddam time here,' said Gruber to Stone, as he toyed with his T-bone steak.

'Yore interview with Lattegan wasn't exactly a roarin' success?' said Stone.

'Nope, the sonofabitch kept his trap well an' truly shut.'

'Ain't that what you expected, Matt?'

'It's exactly what I expected,' growled Gruber morosely. 'I said as much to John Downie when he gave me my orders.'

'But still he sent you?'

'Yeah. To be fair, he had no choice. The US

Government are mighty anxious to git back that money Lattegan stole from the Fort Brandon pay-wagon.' Gruber glanced across the dining-room in the direction of Belle Nightingale. 'Y'know that's Mrs Lattegan sittin' over there?' he said.

'Yup. News spreads fast in this town,' replied Stone.

'Sure does. Anyways, I reckon she's here for the same reason as I am.'

'Could be, Matt, though it's jest possible she's here simply to say farewell to her husband.'

Gruber smiled sourly.

'C'mon, Jack! You ain't that gullible. You know, as well as I do, that kinda woman is out for what she can git.'

'Mebbe.'

Stone returned the marshal's smile, though he felt distinctly unhappy about deceiving him regarding Lattegan's wife. He consoled himself with the thought that Belle was no more likely than Gruber to prise the location of his loot from Lattegan.

'She's a good-lookin' woman, I'll say that for her,' remarked Gruber.

'Yup.'

'I'd invite her to join us, but I don't s'pose that'd be proper in the circumstances?'

'No, I guess not.'

'Anyways, as we've both finished our meal,

hows about goin' through to the bar-room for a few drinks 'fore we turn in?'

'Why not?' said Stone.

It was shortly before midnight when Stone finally turned in. His head had hardly hit the pillow before he was aroused by a tap on his bedroom door. Grabbing his Frontier Model Colt, he crossed the room and cautiously opened the door a fraction. There on the threshold stood Belle Nightingale, clad only in a black silk peignoir. She smiled seductively.

'That ain't no way to greet a lady,' she murmured, eyeing the revolver.

'Sorry, Belle.' The Kentuckian lowered the gun and opened the door sufficiently to permit her entry into the bedroom. 'I ... I wasn't expectin' anyone to call at this hour,' he confessed.

'Past yore bed-time, Jack?' she asked.

'I guess, but I'm wide awake now,' replied Stone.

'Good!' Belle continued to smile seductively. 'I've got me a li'l proposition to put to you, but that can wait a while,' she murmured.

So saying, the blonde slipped the peignoir off her shoulders and stood before him as naked as the day she was born. Stone's eyes hungrily devoured her voluptuous white body, then he pulled her into his arms. They kissed and tumbled into bed. Both, for various reasons, had suffered a long period of abstinence. Consequently, they made up for lost time with a bout of wild, uninhibited lovemaking.

Afterwards, replete, they lay in each other's arms.

'You sure are one helluva woman!' gasped the Kentuckian.

'That was good, huh?' smiled Belle.

'As good as it gits.'

'For me, too.'

'An' you supposed to be the grievin' widow-to-be!'

Belle laughed.

'Jest as well Sheriff Blake cain't see me now,' she remarked.

'You bet.'

'Though mebbe there'll be no grievin'.'

'Whaddya mean?'

'I mean, if Larry don't hang, I won't have to pretend to grieve.'

'Oh, he's gonna hang for certain!'

'Not if he's sprung. Which brings me to that li'l proposition I mentioned earlier.'

'Oh, no!'

'Oh, yes, Jack! We could spring him.'

'We?'

'I cain't do it on my own. But, with some help from you, I figure it could be done.'

'Yo're kiddin'!'

'No, I ain't, Jack. Think of all that loot buried up in the mountains. We git Larry outa that jail an' we split it three ways.'

Stone disengaged himself from Belle's embrace.

'Forget it, Belle,' he growled.

'You . . . you refusin' to help me, Jack?' enquired the blonde.

'I am.'

'But, Jack. . . !'

'I don't want no part of Lattegan's ill-gotten gains, an' I *do* want the murderin' bastard to hang.'

'Aw, come on, Jack!'

'No, Belle; you are on yore own. So, let it be.'

'Why should I?'

'Because, if you try recruitin' someone else to help you, I'll be obliged to tell Matt Gruber that you ain't Lattegan's wife. An', if 'n' he don't run you outa town hisself, I figure he'll git the sheriff to do it.'

'Goddam you, Jack!'

The blonde leapt out of bed and, wrapping her peignoir round her, glared at the Kentuckian with furious, blazing eyes.

'Take it easy, Belle,' he replied quietly. 'Should you succeed in persuadin' Lattegan to divulge where he's hidden his loot *without* springin' him from jail, wa'al, that ain't no concern of mine.'

'He won't say nothin' while he's in that cell.'

74

'Then that's jest too bad.'

'You sonofabitch!'

Belle turned angrily upon her heel and marched out of the bedroom, slamming the door behind her. Stone followed in her footsteps and, pulling open the door, poked his head out.

'I warn yuh not to try anythin', Belle,' he called after her, 'for I'll be keepin' an eye on you. That's a promise.'

'Sonofabitch!' she repeated, and promptly vanished into her bedroom.

Stone smiled wryly. He was extremely glad that Belle hadn't put her proposition *before* they jumped into bed together.

SIX

The morning of 19 June dawned bright and sunny. A despondent Belle Nightingale sat at the window gazing glumly out upon Main Street. There was little traffic since the folks had not yet started arriving for the forthcoming hanging. Some, she reckoned, might turn up during the course of the day, but she expected that most would arrive on the twentieth or on Midsummer Day itself.

The morning passed slowly, with Belle brooding on Jack Stone's refusal to help her and churning over in her mind all sorts of ideas about how she alone might effect Lucky Larry Lattegan's escape. Unfortunately, none of the ideas, when properly thought through, seemed at all feasible.

After lunch in the hotel dining-room, Belle decided she needed a breath of fresh air and so proceeded to stroll round town, paying a second fruitless visit to Lattegan in his cell at the rear of the law-office, peering in several shop windows and entering various stores. She didn't buy anything, however, not because she saw nothing she liked, but because she was pretty low in funds and needed almost every cent she possessed to get her back to Wichita should her enterprise fail.

It was late afternoon and the sun was beginning to sink in the west as Belle emerged from Fred Hope's dry-goods store and made her way slowly back towards the Cougar Creek Hotel. She had almost reached the entrance when she chanced to glance across the street in the direction of the Prairie Dog Saloon. Two riders had dismounted and were in the process of hitching their horses to the rail outside the saloon. And, despite their changed appearance, Belle straightway recognized them as Lattegan's erstwhile confederates, Mad Dog Mel and Joe Flaherty. She watched them enter the saloon.

Why, she wondered, were those two in town? They had to have a very good reason, considering that the last time they had ridden into Cougar Creek it had been in order to rob the bank. Although they had radically altered their looks, Joe Flaherty and the newly bespectacled Mad Dog Mel were taking a considerable risk. If they were recognized, their chances of breaking free a second time would not be good. And, should they be taken, they would surely share Lattegan's fate.

Belle smiled to herself. The only possible reason they could have had for turning up in Cougar Creek at the present time was to engineer their old boss's escape. She determined, therefore, to get in on the act. But how was she to contact the two outlaws without Jack Stone observing her? She had noticed, during her walk round the town, that the Kentuckian was keeping a discreet watch over her movements, as he had promised.

Belle entered the hotel in thoughtful mood. She walked down the reception hall and, as she approached the foot of the stairs, Benny Brooks greeted her.

"Evenin', Mrs Lattegan; had a nice day, I hope?' he said, with an awkward grin.

Belle smiled sweetly at the clerk.

'Benny,' she said, 'I'd like you to do me a li'l favour.'

'Of course, Mrs Lattegan,' he responded eagerly.

'Oh, do call me Belle! I feel we're friends, an' it ain't right friends should be formal with each other, now is it, Benny?'

'Er . . . no . . . no, certainly not, Mrs . . . er . . . Belle.'

'That's better.' Belle continued to dazzle the clerk with her most seductive of smiles, noting the flush of pleasure that transformed his countenance. 'I have a problem, you see,' she confided.

'Yes, Belle?'

'My brother an' my husband's brother are both in town to pay their last respects to Larry. Naturally, I'd like to have a word with them.'

'Naturally,' agreed Benny Brooks.

'But they're both still wanted by the law. They've disguised themselves pretty well, though I reckon that Mr Stone an' Marshal Gruber might still recognize 'em if either should happen to bump into 'em.'

'I see yore problem.'

'Yes. I gotta rendezvous with them some place safe an' outa sight.' Belle sighed and added, 'The only place I can think of is my bedroom.'

'Right.'

'Now, if last night's anythin' to go by, Stone an' the marshal will head for the hotel bar-room straight away after dinner. That, then, would be a good time for my brother an' brother-in-law to pay me a visit. I propose, therefore, to draft a note invitin' them to call at nine o' clock tonight. That'll give us time to have a decent conversation, with them safely gone before Stone an' Gruber even think of leavin' the bar-room. So, will you deliver my note for me, Benny?'

'Willingly, Mrs . . . er . . . Belle.'

'I'll pay you, of course.'

'There's no need.'

'I insist.' Belle fished in her reticule and

produced a five-dollar bill which she slipped to the clerk. 'You'll find them in the Prairie Dog Saloon,' she said.

'How will I recognize 'em?' enquired Benny Brooks.

'They're dressed like a coupla cowpokes, one short an' squat an' with a livid white scar disfigurin' his left cheek, while his companion is of about average height, fairly heavily built, an' with an ugly mug an' sportin' a pair of wire-framed spectacles.'

'That's a pretty fair description.'

'You think you'll find 'em, Benny?'

'Sure thing, Belle.'

'OK, I'll go draft that note.'

Upstairs, in the privacy of her bedroom, the blonde wrote the following few words on a thin sheet of writing paper, which she then folded in two:

Unless you want me to inform the sheriff who you are, be at Room 14 of the Cougar Creek Hotel tonight, at nine o' clock sharp. Belle.

This note Belle handed to Benny Brooks, then she returned to her room.

She stood at the bedroom window and watched the hotel clerk scuttle across the street and into the saloon. A few minutes passed before he reappeared. As he recrossed the street, he glanced up towards Belle's window. He raised both hands and gave a 'thumbs up' sign. Belle responded with a grateful smile and an enthusiastic wave.

The time hung heavily on her hands that evening. Belle delayed going down to dinner until some minutes after she heard Stone leave his room and head off downstairs. Upon arrival in the dining-room, she observed that the Kentuckian was again sharing a table with US Marshal Matt Gruber. She chose a table at the opposite end of the dining-room and sat down. Stone nodded in her direction and then promptly continued his conversation with the marshal.

'So, Matt,' he said, 'you spent the entire afternoon closeted with Lucky Larry Lattegan?'

'That's right,' replied Gruber.

'To no effect?'

'None whatsoever. He talked 'bout everythin' under the sun except the whereabouts of his loot. Seemed eager to talk.'

'Must git lonesome in that cell.'

'I s'pose. Anyways, he won't be confined there for much longer. Another coupla days an' they'll string him up.'

'An' then you can return to Laramie.'

'Yeah. An' you can begin that huntin' trip you planned.'

'I ain't in no partickler hurry, though I'll probably head out jest 'fore the hangin'.'

'So, what did you do this afternoon, Jack, while I was quizzin' Lattegan?'

'Aw, this an' that! Strolled up an' down Main Street a coupla times. Had me a snooze.' Stone could not tell Gruber that he had spent his day keeping a close eye on Belle Nightingale. If he did, he would need to say why and that would likely result in Gruber getting the sheriff to run her out of town. 'It's kinda pleasant doin' next to nothin' for a change,' he concluded.

'Guess so,' agreed Gruber amiably.

As the two men conversed together, Belle kept them under observation, yet without seeming to do so. Also, she timed her meal to keep pace with theirs. And so it was that, when they had drunk their coffee and rose to go, she did likewise. They, all three, reached the dining-room door together, Stone gallantly holding it open while Belle passed through into the lobby.

'Good night, Mrs Lattegan,' he said, as she turned towards the stairs.

'Good night, gentlemen,' she replied.

Half-way up the stairs, she paused and watched the two men enter the hotel bar-room. Belle delved into her reticule and pulled out her watch. The time was exactly half past eight. She smiled. The Kentuckian and the marshal would be safely

out of the way when Mad Dog Mel and Joe
Flaherty called upon her at nine o' clock.

The next half-hour seemed to take an age to
pass, but presently, at precisely two minutes past
nine o'clock, there came a loud knocking upon
Belle's door. She crossed the room and threw open
the door.

'Do come in, gentlemen,' she said.

Two stony-faced desperadoes faced Belle across
the threshold. Neither man looked particularly
pleased to see her. Upon her return to the room,
she had removed her hat and lifted her veil. In
consequence, they had no difficulty in recognizing
her.

'Oh, so it's you!' snarled Mad Dog Mel, looking
very odd behind his lensless spectacles.

'I did sign my note to you,' replied Belle, as she
ushered them into the bedroom.

'You ain't the only Belle in the West,' rasped Joe
Flaherty.

'No, I guess not.'

'We didn't care much for that threat to turn us
in to the sheriff,' said Mad Dog Mel.

'We surely didn't,' affirmed Flaherty.

'I had to put that in my note, to ensure that you
came,' explained Belle. 'But I had no intention of
informin' Sheriff Blake. You have my word on
that,' she added contritely.

'Oh, yeah?' growled Flaherty.

'Yes. Informin' on folks jest ain't my style.'

The two outlaws exchanged glances. They had known Belle pretty well in the days when she was Lucky Larry Lattegan's lover. They did, in fact, believe her.

'OK. Whaddya want?' demanded Mad Dog Mel.

'I know why yo're here in Cougar Creek.'

'Is that so?' Mad Dog Mel glowered.

'Yeah.'

'Tell us, then,' snapped Flaherty.

'Yo're here to help Larry escape jail.'

'Mebbe we jest came to watch him hang,' said Mad Dog Mel.

'I don't think so.'

'An' why would we wanta help him escape?' enquired Flaherty.

'He was yore boss once.'

'We'd need a better reason than that. Gittin' him outa jail ain't gonna be no piece of cake,' commented Flaherty.

'When you git him out, yo're gonna demand he shares out that loot he's buried in the mountains of the Medicine Bow range.'

'You don't believe that ol' rumour, Belle,' sneered Flaherty.

'I do, an' so do you.'

'Aw, come on. . . !'

'You come on, Mad Dog. That's the reason yo're here.'

'An' if 'n' it is?' Mad Dog Mel glared at her.

'I want my share of that loot.'

'Yore share?'

'Yes, Mad Dog. I was as near as dammit married to Larry an' . . .'

'That's ancient history,' said Flaherty.

'Wa'al, then, mebbe I can help you in some way!'

'We don't need yore help.'

'Are you sure about that, Joe?'

'I am.'

'Wa'al, at least tell me what you plan doin'.'

'Why should I?'

'Jest in case there's a flaw in yore plan that you ain't spotted. I don't mean no disrespect, but you fellers ain't exactly used to makin' plans. You always left that to Larry.'

Once again the two outlaws exchanged glances.

'OK,' said Flaherty finally. 'The plan is this: We've got hold of some sticks of dynamite, an' we aim to bury 'em in the earth next to Larry's cell an' blast a hole in the wall. We'll be mounted an' ready to go, with a spare hoss for Larry to ride.'

'Simple, huh?' growled Mad Dog Mel.

'Have you seen the jail?'

'Not yet,' admitted Flaherty.

'We b'lieve it's back of the law-office,' added Mad Dog Mel.

'That's right. It consists of five cells. So, how are yuh gonna find out which one holds Larry?'

85

'When we give them the once-over tomorrow mornin', it's quite likely he'll be lookin' outa his cell window,' declared Mad Dog Mel.

'An' if 'n' he ain't?'

'Wa'al, we'll jest have to mosey on over an' look in through each in turn,' said Flaherty.

'Don't you think that might make you a mite conspicuous?' suggested Belle.

For a third time, the two outlaws exchanged glances.

'I guess it might at that,' conceded Flaherty.

'We can simply dash past, glancin' into each cell as we go by,' remarked Mad Dog Mel.

'But won't you have to alert Larry to yore plan?'

'I don't see why. Once we've blasted a hole in his cell wall, he sure ain't gonna hang about. He'll be outa there in a coupla shakes,' said Mad Dog Mel.

'Not if he happens to be standin' next to the outside wall when the explosion occurs. Then, like as not, he'll be dead,' said Belle.

'Holy cow! I hadn't thought of that!' exclaimed Mad Dog Mel.

'Me neither,' confessed Flaherty.

'If you cut me in, an' that'll mean splittin' Larry's loot four ways, I think I can help,' said the blonde.

'How?' enquired Flaherty.

'I can tell you exactly which cell Larry is occupyin', an' I can git to see him to inform him of our plans.'

86

'How'll you manage that? The sheriff ain't gonna permit Larry no visitors surely?'

'He allows his wife to visit him.'

'But Larry ain't got no wife. He . . . hell, Belle, you been passin' yoreself off as Mrs Lattegan?'

'That's right, Joe. An' I've visited him twice already.'

'OK. Mebbe we should cut you in. Whaddya say, Mad Dog?'

The other outlaw rubbed his jaw thoughtfully.

'It's OK by me, I guess,' he conceded after several moments' contemplation.

Belle smiled.

'Good!' she said. 'Now, tell me, boys, when do you plan to carry out yore dynamitin'?'

'Sometime after dark tomorrow,' said Flaherty.

'Yeah. We'll plant them half-dozen sticks . . .' began Mad Dog Mel.

'Half a dozen sticks of dynamite!' cried Belle.

'Yeah.'

'Goddammit, Mad Dog, you wanta blow up the whole darned cell an' Larry with it?'

'Whaddya mean?'

'I mean, a coupla sticks should prove ample to blow a hole in the cell wall.'

'So, what do we do with the other four sticks?' demanded Flaherty.

'You do nothin' with 'em.' Belle paused as a thought suddenly struck her. Then she continued,

'On second thoughts, I reckon mebbe they could come in useful after all.'

'Oh, yeah?' said Flaherty.

'Yes,' replied Belle, and she went on to explain exactly what she had in mind.

When she had finished, the two desperadoes gazed admiringly at her. Lattegan had been the brains of the outfit. They had merely done his bidding. They badly needed someone to boss them and they had found that someone in Belle Nightingale.

'OK, we'll do as you suggest,' said Flaherty.

'You said you were gonna git a spare hoss for Larry. Wa'al, you'll need to git another for me,' remarked Belle.

'Fine.'

'Shall we meet outside the Prairie Dog Saloon tomorrow night at eight o' clock sharp? Most of Cougar Creek's citizens'll be dinin' at that hour.'

'Right.'

'An', meantime, I'll visit Larry an' let him know our plans.'

'Anythin' else?'

'Yeah, Joe. If 'n' we should happen to pass in the street, we don't know each other.'

'Sure thing, Belle.'

'Wa'al, I guess that 'bout covers everythin'. So, I'll bid you good-night, boys.'

The two outlaws nodded and made for the door.

'Good-night, Belle,' they chorused as they departed.

Once the bedroom door had closed behind them, Belle Nightingale smiled to herself. Her eyes glinted greedily as she thought of what she might do with her share of Lattegan's loot.

Mad Dog Mel and Joe Flaherty, meantime, were crossing Main Street on their way back to the Prairie Dog Saloon. As they clambered up the short flight of wooden steps leading to the stoop outside the saloon, three Arapaho Indians rode past, proceeding slowly along the street in the direction of the law-office.

'Why did you bring us into this town, Spotted Tail?' enquired Wolf That Speaks.

'This town holds an outlaw named Lucky Larry Lattegan. I overheard Curtis speak of him.'

'What is that to us?'

'The outlaw is to be hanged.'

'When is this to happen?'

'Soon, I think. The friend of Curtis, he said there will be a big crowd to see the hanging.'

'We cannot wait. The bluecoats will be searching for us,' remarked Little Elk.

'We camp out on those bluffs overlooking the town,' said Spotted Tail, and he pointed towards some tall cliffs that stood to the south of Cougar Creek. He tapped the binoculars which he had taken from the late lamented Sergeant Bill

McDowd. 'With these we can watch the hanging, and we can also observe the approach of our pursuers, should they pick up our trail.'

'But why wait? What is this hanging to us?' demanded Wolf That Speaks.

Spotted Tail smiled grimly and explained what he had in mind. At the conclusion of his explanation, his two companions said nothing, but simply nodded their heads. Then, upon reaching the law-office, they trotted down the alleyway which ran between it and Fred Hope's dry-goods store. They passed the newly-erected scaffold and paused. They glanced towards the cells at the rear of the law-office. A face peered through the barred windows of the middle cell, but the Indians had no way of knowing whether it was the face of Lucky Larry Lattegan. They urged their horses forward, heading southwards towards the bluffs.

SEVEN

The crowds began to descend upon Cougar Creek on 20 June. Hiram G. Culpepper and the rest of the town council rubbed their hands with glee. The town's saloons, hotels, shops and stores were all enjoying a brisk trade, while the arrival of itinerant medicine-men, fortune-tellers, card-sharps, jugglers, fire-eaters and various other street entertainers gave it something of a carnival atmosphere. As the mayor remarked jocosely, 'Guess the Fourth of July's hit Cougar Creek a li'l early this year!'

Sheriff Jim Blake was rather less delighted, for, amongst the general influx, there was a large number of riff-raff, troublemakers and belligerent drunks to be taken care of. Consequently, he, Deputy Tom Jeffers and the four temporary deputies were kept pretty busy. No longer did Lucky Larry Lattegan have the jail to himself.

During the course of that afternoon and evening, the other four cells were filled. And, while Lattegan remained the sole occupant of the middle cell, the others each held two, or three, or more prisoners.

It was late morning when Bart Kingston and the Cobb brothers eventually rode into town. They halted in front of Sullivan's Saloon on the edge of Cougar Creek. They hitched their horses to the rail outside and went in through the batwing doors. The bar, with its hammered copper bar-top, ran the length of one side of the narrow rectangular-shaped room. A few unlit brass lamps hung from the rafters and the floor was sprinkled with sawdust. Bart Kingston tossed the remains of his cigar into the spittoon and lit a fresh one. He ordered three beers, which they took to a table beside the window overlooking Main Street.

'OK, boys,' he said, 'I figure we'd best split up while we look for Joe Flaherty an' Mad Dog Mel. An', remember, we sure as hell don't want them to spot us.'

'We'll jest melt into the crowd, won't we, Jake?' said Gil Cobb.

'Sure thing,' asserted his brother.

'Yeah. Wa'al, be certain that you do,' snapped Kingston.

'What are we s'posed to do then, when we find 'em?' asked Jake Cobb.

'Make a note of whereabouts they're hangin' out an' head back here. We'll take it from there.'

'You got a plan, boss?' enquired Gil Cobb.

'Yeah. Kind of.' Bart Kingston smiled wryly. He was in two minds. He didn't know whether to challenge Mad Dog Mel and Joe Flaherty and demand a piece of the action, or simply to keep them under surveillance and step in only when the time seemed ripe. 'I'll decide what we do after we've discovered where they're hangin' out,' he growled.

'How long do we keep lookin' for 'em?' said Gil Cobb.

'Whaddya mean?'

'I mean, boss, if, say, we ain't found 'em in three hours' time, are we expected to carry on the search?'

'No. Give it a coupla hours at most. If 'n' you ain't found 'em by then, report back here anyway.'

'OK.'

'You boys check the crowds formed round the various street attractions, an' also check the eatin'-houses an' the saloons. Gil, you take the south side of the street an' Jake, you take the north side. Me, I'll check up on the hotels an' the several stores in town,' said Bart Kingston.

Shortly after noon Belle Nightingale tapped on Jack Stone's bedroom door. The Kentuckian had been observing Main Street from his window, since he had no intention of permitting Belle to leave the hotel and roam freely about town. He wanted to be sure she was making no secret arrangements to spring Lattegan. He was surprised, therefore, to find the blonde standing in his doorway.

She was still clad in her widow's weeds, but she had lifted the veil. She graced Stone with her most winning smile.

'Howdy, Jack. Surprised to see me?' she asked.

'Wa'al, after the other night. . . .'

'I've been thinkin' 'bout that, Jack. Springin' Larry from jail wouldn't be no easy task. Like as not, anyone who tried would end up gittin' hisself shot.'

'Or herself.'

'Yeah. So, that's what I wanted to tell you. I've given up the idea. I'm gonna keep on visitin' Larry right up until they hang him. Mebbe, after all, I can persuade him to divulge whereabouts he's hidden his loot.'

'If 'n' you do, that's yore affair, Belle. Like I said the other night, it ain't no concern of mine.'

'So, you won't split on me to Marshal Gruber?'

'Not unless you step outa line.'

'I won't, Jack; I promise you.' Belle continued to smile seductively. 'It was good in bed, wasn't it?' she murmured.

94

'Sure was,' grinned Stone.

'We could do it again. Tonight, after supper.'

'OK.'

'I'll tap on yore door like last time.'

'I shall look forward to it, Belle,' said the Kentuckian. Then he asked, 'You on yore way to visit Lattegan?'

'Yeah.'

'Wa'al, good luck.'

'Thanks, Jack.'

'Till tonight, then.'

'Till tonight.'

Belle dropped her veil and retreated downstairs. She exchanged a friendly greeting with Benny Brooks in the lobby, then left the hotel and headed along the sidewalk towards the law-office.

By chance, she was spotted entering the law-office by Bart Kingston as he emerged from Fred Hope's emporium. He strolled over to where Deputy Sheriff Tom Jeffers was standing on the stoop outside, idly smoking a cheroot.

'Pardon me, Deppity,' he said, 'but can you tell me who that widow woman was, steppin' into yore office?'

'What's it to you?' enquired the young deputy.

'Jest idle curiosity,' said Kingston. 'There was somethin' familiar 'bout her. I wondered if I knew her from somewhere.'

'Wa'al, in the first place, she ain't no widow.'

'No?'

'No. Not yet, leastways.'

'Whaddya mean?'

'I mean, she soon will be. Shortly after eleven tomorrow mornin' in fact. She's Lucky Larry Lattegan's ever-lovin' wife.'

'You don't say!'

'I do.'

'Wa'al, thanks, Deppity. I guess I must've been mistaken when I thought I knew her. I ain't acquainted with no Mrs Lattegan.'

Bart Kingston crossed the street and entered Ma Cheney's Eating-house. He sat himself down at a table by the window and ordered coffee and a plate of eggs and beans with rye bread. Then he waited and watched. He had spoken the truth when he had said he wasn't acquainted with Mrs Lattegan. Indeed, he was unaware that Lattegan had ever married. But his curiosity was roused. Was Mrs Lattegan in Cougar Creek simply in order to say her fond farewells to her husband? Or was she, too, here to discover the whereabouts of his loot? Kingston decided at least to find out where in Cougar Creek she was staying. His search for Joe Flaherty and Mad Dog Mel was temporarily suspended.

Meantime, Belle was once again in the rear quarters of the law-office, confronting Lattegan in his cell. She was put out to discover that the adjoining cells also contained prisoners, most of whom were in a drunken stupor.

'Hi, Larry, how's it goin'?' enquired Belle, when the door between the cells and the outer office had closed and Sheriff Jim Blake departed.

'How'd yuh think it's goin'?' growled Lattegan sourly.

'Not too good, huh?'

'Waitin' to be hanged ain't a lotta fun, Belle.'

'Mebbe you ain't gonna be hanged.'

'Whaddya mean?'

Belle lowered her voice to a whisper.

'You said, if 'n I spring you, you'd share that loot you got stashed away with me.'

'So I did, Belle.' Lattegan's eyes gleamed. 'You gotta plan to git me outa here?' he enquired quietly.

'Yeah. Only I cain't do it on my own,' murmured Belle.

'So?'

'So, yo're gonna have to split that money four ways.'

'You have a coupla pardners?'

'That's right, Larry.'

'I hope they're up to the job?'

'I think they'll do. They're the survivin' members of yore ol' gang.'

'Joe an' Mad Dog?'

'The same.'

Lattegan grinned.

'So, what's the plan?'

'We're gonna blow a hole in that there wall.' Belle indicated the outside wall of Lattegan's cell with a quick nod of the head. 'The three of us'll be waitin' outside with a spare hoss for you.'

'What about the sheriff an' his deppity?'

'Don't worry 'bout them. They're gonna be occupied elsewhere. By the time they git back here, we'll be gone.'

'That sounds good. So, what time is this here break-out gonna take place?'

'Shortly after eight this evenin'. Now you be sure to stay well away from that outside wall,' Belle warned the outlaw, her voice still no more than a whisper.

'You bet I will,' said Lattegan.

'An', once we're sure we've shook off any pursuin' posse, you'll take us to the spot in the mountains where you've buried yore loot?'

'Yup.'

'An' you'll split it four ways?'

'That's the deal, ain't it?'

'It is.'

'Then, you have my word, Belle.'

'OK, Larry.' Belle smiled happily. She leaned forward and kissed him through the bars. 'We'll have ourselves a real good time once we git you outa here,' she remarked softly.

'We sure will,' replied Lattegan.

'Until this evenin', then, Larry,' she whispered.

'Yeah. I'll be ready an' waitin'.'

"Bye, Larry,' she said, reverting to her usual voice.

"Bye, Belle.'

The blonde dropped her veil and returned to the outer office. She exchanged a few words with the sheriff, whose turn it was to man the law-office. Then she stepped outside and made her way slowly back towards the hotel.

Bart Kingston observed Belle's reappearance from his vantage-point in Ma Cheney's Eating-house. He quickly downed the remains of his coffee, paid his bill and hurried outside. A fast walk along the sidewalk soon brought him level with Belle, who continued to stroll in leisurely fashion on the opposite side of the street. He slackened his pace to match the blonde's and ambled along at this much-reduced speed until presently Belle reached the Cougar Creek Hotel and vanished inside its portals. Kingston grinned broadly and promptly headed for Sullivan's Saloon.

There he found the Cobb brothers sitting drinking beer at the same table they had occupied earlier.

'Wa'al, boys, did you find them two varmints?' he enquired eagerly.

'Sure did, boss,' replied Jake Cobb.

'Yeah. They're hangin' out at the Prairie Dog Saloon,' added his brother.

'S'pose they ain't plannin' to spring Lattegan. S'pose . . .' began Jake Cobb.

'What in tarnation do they want that dynamite they purchased off Phil Campbell for, if 'n' it ain't to blast a hole in Lattegan's cell wall? C'mon, Jake, that's gotta be why they're here in Cougar Creek!' exclaimed the saloonkeeper.

'Wa'al, yeah; I . . . I guess so, boss.'

'So, I want you fellers to keep an eye on 'em.'

'But, if we hang out at the Prairie Dog, they're sure to spot us,' protested Gil Cobb.

'Together, mebbe. But, if you take it in turns an' keep as far away from our quarry as you can, you should escape their notice. I mean, the saloon's pretty darned crowded, ain't it?'

'That's true. The town's jam-packed with folks comin' to see tomorrow's hangin', an' the Prairie Dog's doin' a roarin' trade,' commented Jake Cobb.

'Wa'al, there you are, then. One of you goes in an' has a beer while the other stays outside on the stoop. You can change over 'bout every hour. Oh, an' don't drink too much beer, for yo're gonna need yore wits about you!'

The Cobb brothers exchanged glances.

'OK,' said Jake Cobb. 'But what the hell do we do if the two of 'em up an' leave the saloon?'

'One of you follows at a discreet distance, while the other reports to me.'

'An' where are you gonna be? Back here?' demanded Gil Cobb.

'Nope. I'll be directly across the street in the Cougar Creek Hotel. You'll find me in either the bar-room or the dinin'-room.' Bart Kingston smiled and continued, 'There's a Mrs Lattegan in town. I aim to keep her under surveillance. Just in case.'

'Hell, I didn't know Lucky Larry Lattegan was married!' exclaimed Jake Cobb.

'Me neither,' said his brother.

'Nor did I till today,' confessed Kingston. 'Anyways, if she's up to somethin', I wanta know exactly what it is.'

'You figure she's gonna try an' spring her husband?'

'I dunno, Jake. Mebbe.'

'She could be in league with Joe Flaherty an' Mad Dog Mel.'

'Could be, Gil.'

'So, for how long do we keep an eye on 'em, boss? Till midnight? Till dawn? Or. . . ?'

'For as long as it takes, Jake,' said Kingston, and he added drily, 'However, it sure as blazes won't be necessary after eleven o'clock tomorrow mornin'.'

'No?' said Gill Cobb.

'Nope; for that's the time they reckon they're gonna hang that sonofabitch, Lattegan.'

With these words, Bart Kingston rose and left Sullivan's Saloon, heading back towards the Cougar Creek Hotel. As for the Cobb brothers, they hastily threw back their beers and made their way along the opposite side of the street in the direction of the Prairie Dog Saloon. Once outside, they tossed a coin to determine who took first watch inside. Jake Cobb won and chose to go inside, whereupon Gil Cobb sat down on the steps leading up the stoop and lit a cheroot.

Bart Kingston had, in the meantime, entered the hotel and engaged a room. After he had had a quick wash, he made his way downstairs to the bar-room. It was about half full. The customers were mainly out-of-towners, who had ridden in to see Lucky Larry Lattegan swing. Of 'Mrs Lattegan', however, there was no sign. Kingston mounted a bar-stool and ordered a beer. He reflected that he would have to take care to pace himself, as he had warned the Cobb brothers to do, for he, too, would need to be in full control of his wits.

The afternoon wore on and Kingston got into conversation with a garrulous dry-goods salesman. He found the man's blather distinctly uninteresting, but at least it helped a little to pass the weary hours. Eventually, though, supper-time arrived.

Bart Kingston followed Jack Stone and US Marshal Matt Gruber into the dining-room. He chose a table at the far side of the room and sat down. His drinking companion remained in the bar-room. He watched as the hotel's customers trooped in to eat. Still there was no sign of 'Mrs Lattegan'.

It was a few minutes past eight and Kingston was toying with a particularly large and remarkably tough steak when the first explosion occurred.

EIGHT

Belle Nightingale took off her black bonnet and gown and donned a check shirt, brown leather vest and Levis. She exchanged her shoes for boots and pinned up her hair. Then she removed a low-crowned black Stetson from her suitcase and clapped it on to her head. Next she strapped on a gunbelt and holster and, after rummaging through the remaining clothes in her suitcase, withdrew a Colt Peacemaker, which she slipped into the holster.

She smiled to herself. She was ready. Checking the ancient timepiece she had won at a poker game in Houston, Texas, she noted that it was one minute to eight o' clock. Time to go!

Belle headed downstairs to find Benny Brooks in his customary position behind the reception desk.

"Evenin' Benny,' she murmured, smiling seductively at the clerk.

'Oh . . . er . . . evenin', Mrs . . . er . . . Belle!' he stammered.

'I expect yo're wonderin' why I'm dressed like this?' she said.

'Er . . . yes . . . yes, I am, as a matter of fact,' replied Benny Brooks, before adding hastily, 'Not that it's any of my business, of course.'

'I'll tell you anyway,' whispered Belle, leaning across the desk until their faces almost touched. 'It's my brother an' brother-in-law. They want me to go with them to the rear of the law-office, where they intend to have a last few words with Larry. It's gonna be kinda tricky an' I jest thought I'd be a li'l less conspicuous dressed up as a cowpoke.'

'I . . . I see.'

'So, I'd 'preciate it if you'd be a pal an' not tell anyone you saw me.'

The blonde's smile widened and her eyes stared wistfully into the clerk's. Benny Brooks was captivated.

'I . . . I won't breathe a word, Belle,' he promised fervently.

'Thank you, Benny. I knew I could rely on you.' So saying, Belle planted a kiss on his lips and then slipped two five-dollar bills across the desk. 'Jest to show my appreciation,' she murmured huskily.

'You . . . you needn't have,' muttered Benny Brooks, but nevertheless he scooped them up and stuffed them into his pocket.

'I'll see you later,' said Belle, although, if every-thing went according to plan, she hoped never again to set foot in Cougar Creek.

'Er . . . yes. Evenin', Belle,' replied the clerk.

He watched the blonde leave the hotel. He did not know whether to believe her story. But she was a lovely looking woman and a generous one, and what was it to do with him? He had promised to keep her secret and he would do just that.

Belle glanced into the dining-room on her way out, and observed Jack Stone and Matt Gruber dining together again at the same table they had occupied on the previous evening. Neither man saw her as she slipped past. Neither, for that matter, did Bart Kingston.

Mad Dog Mel and Joe Flaherty were waiting for her on the stoop in front of the Prairie Dog Saloon.

'OK,' she said briskly. 'You got everythin' you need?'

'We sure have,' replied Joe Flaherty. 'The sticks of dynamite, the fulminate caps an' the fuse.'

'You've cut the fuse into three equal lengths?'

'That's right, Belle. Jest as you told us.'

'Good. An' you know what to do, Joe?

'Trust me.'

'If 'n' I'd trusted you straight off, you'd've blown Larry to kingdom come!'

106

'OK, so I ain't no explosives expert. But I ain't stoopid; I can light a fuse as well as the next man.'

'I'm sure you can, but, anyways, I'll run over the plan one last time. I don't want no mistakes.'

'I'm listenin', Belle.'

'Me, too,' added Mad Dog Mel.

'Right. This is how we do it. The livery stables are at the western end of Main Street an' the stockyards at the eastern end. You, Joe, go lay a coupla sticks up against the side of the stables, then another couple close by the stockyards, an' finally the last couple up against the wall of Larry's cell, the middle one of the five cells. Got that?'

'Got it.'

'Good! Where are the hosses, by the way?'

'Hitched to the rail there.' Flaherty pointed to the hitching rail in front of the saloon.

'Those four?'

'Yup.'

'OK, Joe. When you've laid the last coupla sticks of dynamite, you report back here, to the saloon. Me an' Mad Dog'll be inside havin' ourselves a drink. Immediately you git back, we leap into action. You boys both got lucifers?'

The two desperadoes nodded.

'Then, you go light the fuse at the livery stables, Joe, while you light the one at the stockyards, Mad Dog. That done, you head for the rear of the law-office, Joe, an' light the fuse there. As for you, Mad Dog, you will return here an', between us, you an' me'll lead those there hosses across Main Street an' down the alley between the law-office an' that dry-goods store. We'll hold 'em there until the dynamite blasts a hole in Larry's cell wall. At which point, we leave the alley an' all of us, includin' Larry, mount up an' hightail it outa town. Is that quite clear?'

'Perfectly,' said Joe Flaherty.

Mad Dog Mel merely nodded.

'Off you go then, Joe,' said Belle.

Flaherty nodded and promptly picked up the small carpet-bag in which he had placed the sticks of dynamite, the fulminate caps and the three lengths of fuse. He turned on his heel and set off along the sidewalk in the direction of the livery stables. He was thankful for the darkness that shrouded Cougar Creek, only punctuated here and there by odd shafts of yellow light spilling out of an occasional doorway or window. No such illumination lit up either the livery stables or the stockyards.

Belle and Mad Dog Mel, meantime, pushed back the batwing doors and entered the saloon. Mad Dog Mel ordered a couple of whiskeys, which they took to a small corner table near the door. Unnoticed by them and lurking among the crowd at the far end of the bar-counter were the Cobb brothers. Jake Cobb had been inside, keeping an eye on the two outlaws, while his brother had been sitting outside on the steps in front of the saloon, patiently smoking a cheroot. Following the outlaws' rendezvous with Belle Nightingale, Gil Cobb had slipped past the three conspirators and joined his brother inside the saloon.

'What in tarnation do we do now?' growled Jake Cobb.

'If either one of us tries to leave to alert the boss, he'll be spotted for sure,' replied Gil Cobb, glancing across towards the corner table. Mad Dog Mel had his back to the crowd, but Belle Nightingale could scarcely help but observe anyone walking out through the batwing doors.

'So, what *do* we do?' demanded Jake Cobb.

'We sit tight an' wait,' remarked his brother glumly.

In the event, they did not have long to wait. Within a quarter of an hour, Joe Flaherty returned and joined his co-conspirators at the corner table. A few brief words were exchanged and then Mad Dog Mel and Flaherty rose and vanished outside into the night. Belle, however, made no move. She continued to sit and sip her whiskey. The Cobb brothers, who had begun to thread their way through the bar-room crowd, halted.

'Goddammit!' snarled Jake Cobb. 'What's goin' on now?'

'Yore guess is as good as mine,' rasped Gil Cobb.
'Do we wait?'

'You got a better idea, Jake?'

'Nope.'

'Then we wait.'

'Hell!'

Again their wait was of no more than a few
minutes' duration. Mad Dog Mel suddenly reappeared and, followed by the blonde, promptly
disappeared again. Immediately, the Cobb brothers pushed their way through the crowd and
dashed outside on to the stoop. They arrived just
in time to observe the shadowy figures of their
quarry cross Main Street and hurry down the
alleyway next to the law-office. The man and the
woman, they noted, were each leading a couple of
horses by their bridles.

'Let's go tell the boss!' cried Jake Cobb.

The brothers were half-way across the street
when the comparative quiet of the evening was
rent by a terrific explosion. This occurred at the
western end of the town and, only a few seconds
later, yet another occurred at the opposite end of
Main Street.

These explosions created exactly the diversion
that Belle had intended. Citizens poured out on
to the street and, joined by those enjoying the
various street entertainments, ran this way and
that.

Among those who hurried towards the livery stables were Hiram G. Culpepper, Dan Mason and Fred Hope. They, together with their wives, had been dining at the mayor's house. Just behind them came Sheriff Jim Blake and three of the four recently-recruited deputies, all of whom had been engaged upon their rounds at the time of this first explosion.

Meantime, hurrying in the direction of the stockyards were the bank manager, Warren Gilchrist, the storekeeper, Lou Anderson, Deputy Sheriff Tom Jeffers and the remaining temporary deputy. Jeffers and his fellow deputy raced towards the scene of the second explosion direct from the law-office, which they had been minding in Sheriff Blake's absence. They passed Bart Kingston and the Cobb brothers, huddled together outside the Cougar Creek Hotel.

Kingston and his hired guns straightway headed for the alleyway down which Belle and Mad Dog Mel had disappeared. They had barely turned into it when a third explosion rent the air, this time emanating from the rear of the law-office.

As the dust slowly settled, Belle Nightingale could see that a large part of the cell wall had been demolished. Coughing and spluttering, Lucky Larry Lattegan emerged through the resulting hole and, beating the dust from his

111

clothes with his hat, hurried towards the blonde and her two companions.

'Holy cow, am I glad to see you!' he ejaculated.

'Hi, boss!' cried Joe Flaherty and Mad Dog Mel in unison.

'I told you I'd git yuh outa there,' said Belle.

'Yeah. Wa'al, let's lam outa this one-hoss town!' exclaimed Lattegan, and he quickly took hold of the reins of one of the horses held by Belle.

'Not so fast,' said a voice from behind him.

Lattegan turned to observe Bart Kingston and the Cobb brothers emerging from the alley. He eyed them keenly.

'You ain't the law,' he rasped.

'No, we ain't,' agreed Kingston amiably. 'We're just some fellers who want a share of yore loot. You wanta lam outa town? Wa'al, we're comin' with you.'

'Is that a fact?' enquired Lattegan.

As he spoke, the outlaw leant towards Belle and, in one lightning-fast movement, pulled the Colt Peacemaker from the blonde's holster, aimed and fired. Fortunately for Bart Kingston, the speed of Lattegan's draw was not matched by its accuracy. The bullet whistled through the saloon-keeper's hair and whipped off his black derby hat. Immediately, Kingston threw himself down on to the ground. Behind him, the Cobb brothers went for their guns.

The gunfight was of short but bloody duration. Mad Dog Mel and Jake Cobb fired simultaneously. Mad Dog Mel's shot struck Jake Cobb in the right temple, exiting through the back of his skull in a cloud of blood and brains, while Cobb's bullet hit the outlaw in the left shoulder and knocked him flat on his back. As for Joe Flaherty, his shot was wide of its target and he took two slugs from Gil Cobb, one in the belly and the other in the chest. Coughing up blood, he sank to his knees, then toppled face downwards and lay twitching in the dust. Meantime, Lattegan had again taken aim. His second shot demolished Gil Cobb's Adam's apple, while his third entered the gunslinger's left eye and exploded inside his brain.

As the gunsmoke cleared, Lattegan stuck the Colt Peacemaker into his belt and, turning to the blonde, snapped, 'OK, Belle, let's git the hell outa here.'

'What about Joe an' Mad Dog?' exclaimed the blonde.

Lattegan shrugged his shoulders.

'Joe's as good as dead an' Mad Dog ain't goin' nowhere,' he retorted. 'So, you comin' or not?'

'I'm comin'!' said Belle.

They quickly mounted and then, without further delay, galloped off towards the bluffs that overlooked Cougar Creek to the south.

As they vanished into the night, US Marshal Matt Gruber and Jack Stone came dashing out of the alley. The marshal loosed off a couple of shots, but more in hope than expectation, for the two riders were already beyond the range of his revolver.

'Goddammit!' he cried. 'The sonofabitch has cheated the rope after all! An' who in blue blazes was that ridin' with him?'

'God knows!' replied Stone, although, despite her disguise, he had recognized the shapely figure of Belle Nightingale. He cursed beneath his breath. He had been taken for a gullible fool. Belle's soft words earlier had been designed to flatter and dupe him, and he had been stupidly expecting her to appear in the hotel dining-room right up until the first explosion. 'God knows!' he repeated dully.

'Then let's ask them,' said Gruber, nodding towards Mad Dog Mel, who lay groaning in the dust, and then at Bart Kingston, who, now that the shooting had ceased, was cautiously rising to his feet.

Of the others, the Cobb brothers were evidently dead, while Joe Flaherty continued to twitch for some moments before eventually, following one final shudder, he lay quite still.

'Looks like yore luck ran out, Mad Dog,' sneered Gruber.

'But Larry's didn't,' growled the outlaw.

'No. Lucky Larry Lattegan. He was well named. So, who was that feller that rode off with him, huh?'

'I ain't sayin'.'

'No?'

'No.'

'He was a youngster. Not much more'n a boy,' volunteered Bart Kingston. He stepped forward and extended his hand. 'Bart Kingston at yore service, Marshal.'

'An' jest what were you doin' here, Mr Kingston?' enquired Gruber, who immediately recognized the owner of Laramie's Hot Spot Saloon.

'The ... er ... the explosion. We was wonderin' 'bout the first two, when we heard a third one. We came to investigate an' observed the outlaw, Lattegan, on the point of escapin'. Naturally, as good citizens, we attempted to prevent him.' Kingston sighed and added, 'Sadly, this public-spirited action cost my friends their lives.'

Mad Dog Mel laughed harshly.

'You goddam liar!' he cried, and, staring up at the marshal, he stated bluntly, 'That sonofabitch an' his pals came here lookin' to share Larry's loot, only Larry wasn't havin' any.'

Gruber turned to Kingston.

'Wa'al, Mr Kingston?' he rasped.

'You . . . you ain't gonna b'lieve that . . . that no-account critter's word against mine, are yuh?' he demanded.

'He ain't got no reason to lie,' interjected Stone.

'That's right,' said Gruber.

'If . . . if that's what you think, then I . . . I'll go. I ain't stayin' around here to be insulted,' blustered Kingston and, with as much dignity as he could muster, he headed off back up the alley.

He was almost bowled over, however, as several others dashed to the scene. Among them were Sheriff Jim Blake, Deputy Tom Jeffers, their four temporary colleagues, Hiram G. Culpepper, Dan Mason and a number of the town's dignitaries.

'What . . . what the hell's goin' on?' demanded Jim Blake, as he surveyed the four prostrate figures, of whom only Mad Dog Mel remained alive.

'Yore bird has flown,' Gruber informed him.

Blake peered at the huge hole in the cell wall and gasped.

'Darn it!' he cried.

'How . . . how did it happen?' asked Culpepper.

'Those two an' some kid, they engineered the explosions an' sprung Lattegan. He an the kid rode off southwards,' said Gruber.

'Southwards?' snapped Blake.

'Yeah.' Gruber pointed towards the bluffs.

'With some kid, you say. A member of Lattegan's old gang?'

'Mebbe. I dunno, Sheriff.' Gruber looked down at Mad Dog Mel, still spread-eagled in the dust. 'This here's one, anyways,' he said.

Jim Blake fixed the outlaw with a stony stare.

'Wa'al, wa'al, Mad Dog Mel!' he said. 'You hurtin' bad? I *do* hope so. But don't worry, we'll git you patched up real good so's you can stand trial. An' nobody ain't gonna be breakin' you outa jail, since you don't have no loot stashed away.'

'Aw, go to hell!' snarled the outlaw.

Sheriff Blake smiled coldly and turned to his deputy.

'Tom,' he said, 'you take this lunkhead an' dump him in a cell. On his own. If 'n' you have to chuck out the present occupants, do it. An' git Doc Chalmers across to have a look at him. OK?'

'Yessir,' said Jeffers.

'The rest of you I'm swearin' in as deppities to ride with me in a posse after Lattegan. You willin'?' demanded Blake.

'We surely are!' declared the mayor enthusiastically.

'Yeah. Let's git goin'!' yelled Luke Barnard, the blacksmith's son.

'You joinin' us, marshal?' the sheriff asked Gruber.

'You headin' south?' Gruber enquired.

'That's the direction Lattegan took, ain't it?' replied Blake.

117

'It is,' said Gruber.

'Then, that's the direction we're takin',' declared Blake.

'Wa'al, I figure Lattegan will eventually veer round to the north. Y'see . . .'

'I ain't interested in yore conjectures, Marshal. Lattegan went south an' that's where we're headin'.'

Gruber smiled thinly and shrugged his shoulders.

'OK, sheriff, you do that,' he said, 'but I won't be joinin' you.'

'Me neither,' said Stone.

Thereupon, the marshal and the Kentuckian headed towards the livery stables, while the others dispersed to find and saddle their horses.

In the event, Gruber and Stone were mounted some minutes before the posse was formed and ready to ride.

'You ridin' with me, Jack?' asked Gruber.

'I guess so. I ain't gonna quit at this stage,' commented Stone.

'But we ain't gonna ride south like the posse, are we?' said Gruber, with a sly grin.

'Nope. We head north towards the Medicine Bow range, where it's rumoured Lattegan has hid his loot,' said the Kentuckian.

As the marshal and the Kentuckian rode off northwards and the posse prepared to ride south,

Bart Kingston sat in the bar-room of the Cougar Creek Hotel and nursed a very large whiskey. He was in a foul temper. His hopes of grabbing a share of Lucky Larry Lattegan's hidden loot were dashed, he had lost his two hired guns, and he expected that, back in Laramie, Baldy Harris was, in all probability, ripping him off. The sooner he returned to the Hot Spot Saloon the better. He cursed his rashness in attempting such a crazy venture. He must have been mad even to contemplate it!

NINE

It was mid-morning on 21 June; Midsummer Day and Lucky Larry Lattegan's fortieth birthday. He and Belle Nightingale had ridden through the night and had finally reached the foothills of the Medicine Bow range. The mountains loomed in front of them, vast, majestic and seeming to reach up into the very heavens. They approached the foothills, one of which vaguely resembled the head of a male African lion. It was, for this reason, known locally as the Lion's Head.

Lattegan led the way up a tortuous zigzag path that wound its way to the summit of the Lion's Head. At the top was a relatively flat plateau in the centre of which had been erected a small cairn.

'OK,' said Lattegan, 'this is it.'

'It's a pity Joe an' Mad Dog didn't make it,' remarked Belle.

'Is it? At least this way we don't have to split the money four ways,' retorted the outlaw.

'That ain't very nice, Larry, considerin' it was them who sprung you,' said Belle.

'Wa'al, mebbe I ain't exactly a nice kinda feller.' Lattegan smiled sourly and added, 'Let's git to it.'

They dismounted and stepped up to the cairn. Lattegan began to remove the stones. He glanced across at the blonde.

'You want yore share, you better start gittin' yore hands dirty,' he rasped.

'You want *me* to move them stones?' she gasped.

'That's right,' he replied.

Belle regarded the cairn with a reluctant eye, but nevertheless began to help Lattegan dismantle it. This took them some little time. Eventually, however, the last stone was tossed aside and Lattegan crouched down. He pulled up three large squares of turf which had been buried beneath the stones. A rectangular hole was revealed.

In this hole lay a canvas bag and, beneath it, four saddle-bags. Lattegan removed the canvas bag, loosened the cord that held it closed and, from inside the bag, produced a gunbelt. A Colt Peacemaker rested in the holster attached to the gunbelt. Lattegan strapped this on, though retaining the revolver he had taken from Belle. That gun remained stuck firmly in his belt.

He then delved one last time into the bag and

came up with an evil-looking, double-edged knife. This he proceeded to slide into the top of one of his boots.

Having thus armed himself, Lattegan opened one of the four saddle-bags, from which he withdrew a large wad of ten-dollar bills. He laughed harshly.

'Are all four of them saddle-bags full of money?' enquired Belle eagerly.

Lattegan nodded and grinned. It was a wolfish grin, the outlaw's cold, coal-black eyes devoid of any hint of humour.

'Indeed they are,' he said.

'Holy cow!'

'Let's sling one pair of saddle-bags on to my hoss an' the other pair on to yours,' he said.

'Sure thing, Larry,' agreed Belle.

The blonde was surprised at the weight of the saddle-bags, but managed, with an effort, to sling them across the back of her roan. This accomplished, she turned to find herself staring down the barrel of a gun.

Lattegan aimed one of his two Colts at Belle's head. He smiled malevolently. Belle gaped into the muzzle while the colour slowly drained from her face.

'What . . . what in tarnation d'yuh think yo're doin'?' she gasped.

'You didn't really think I was gonna share my

loot with you, did yuh?' he retorted.

'But . . . but I played my part in gittin' you outa jail!' she exclaimed. ''Deed, those two lunkheads would never have managed without me to instruct 'em.'

'Is that a fact?'

'It is, Larry. You know what they were like. They've always needed someone to tell 'em what to do.'

'That's true.'

'So . . . so, surely a li'l gratitude is in order?'

'I don't give a damn what is or ain't in order.'

'Aw, come on!' Belle cried in desperation. 'You don't need to split it down the middle. I . . . I'll be content with . . .'

'Nothin'.'

'No! No, Larry, that ain't fair!'

'Who cares if it ain't fair?'

'I do.'

'Wa'al, I don't, Belle, an' I'm the one holdin' the gun.'

'So, what are yuh gonna do, Larry? Jest ride off an leave me here?'

'That's about it.'

'But this . . . this is wild country! You cain't leave me unarmed an' without a hoss! I mean, s'pose a grizzly, or a cougar, or. . . ?'

'You don't have to worry 'bout no wild animal, Belle.'

'No?'

'Nope.' Lattegan thumbed back the hammer and lowered his aim so that the revolver pointed directly at Belle's heart. 'See, yo're gonna be dead long 'fore any four-legged critter chances upon you.'

'You . . . you don't have to shoot me, Larry!' shouted the girl.

'Oh, I think I do!' replied Lattegan.

'But why?' demanded Belle. 'I ain't no threat to you.'

'If I leave you an' the posse, which is sure to be out lookin' for us, comes across you, you could tell 'em the direction I took.'

'I wouldn't do that! Honest I wouldn't, Larry!'

'Sorry, Belle, but that ain't a risk I'm prepared to take.'

'No! Please, Larry, don't kill me! For God's sake. . . !'

As Belle pleaded for her life, a voice suddenly rang out.

'He will kill nobody, white woman.'

Both Belle and Lattegan turned their heads. So preoccupied had they been, they had failed to observe the arrival of the three Arapaho Indians, who had ridden quietly up on to the plateau and now rode forward to confront them.

Spotted Tail and his two companions sat astride their horses, their guns trained on the outlaw. From his vantage-point above Cougar

Creek, Spotted Tail had, with the aid of the late Sergeant Bill McDowd's binoculars, observed Lattegan make his escape. The Arapahos had promptly set off in pursuit and had stayed on Lattegan's trail all the way to the foothills of the Medicine Bow range. They had, however, taken all the necessary precautions to ensure that the outlaw remained unaware of their presence.

'This ain't none of yore goddam business,' snarled Lattegan.

'We are making it our business,' replied Spotted Tail.

'Now, listen, you red sonsofabitch. . . !' exclaimed the outlaw.

'No. You listen, Mr Lattegan,' said Spotted Tail.

Lucky Larry Lattegan's jaw dropped.

'How in blue blazes d'yuh know my name?' he demanded.

'We know all about you. About your escape from jail. About the money hidden in those four saddlebags.'

'I . . . I earned that money!'

'You stole it.'

'Whatever. It's mine.'

'Was yours.'

'Hell, it ain't no use to you!'

'You think not?'

'No. I mean, it's pretty darned plain you three fellers have fled from some reservation or other.'

'So?'

'So, yo're gonna lose yoreselves someplace deep in the forests or up in the mountains. Do a li'l huntin' an' trappin'. Across the border in Canada, if I guess right.'

'You do.'

'Wa'al, you ain't gonna have no use there for all the loot I got. I can let you have a few dollars to buy some ammunition or guns. That's all yo're likely to need, surely?'

'For ourselves, yes.'

'Wa'al, who else is involved, for Pete's sake?'

'Our people back on the reservation.'

'Yes, it is for their sake that we are here,' added Wolf That Speaks.

This was true. Spotted Tail had told his two companions of the conversation he had overheard in Rex Curtis's trading post. He had gone on to suggest that they wait on the bluffs overlooking Cougar Creek in case, as had eventually happened, Lattegan's confederates tried and succeeded in breaking him out of jail. Then Spotted Tail had argued, they could let the outlaw lead them to where he had stashed his loot, take it off him and hand it over to Chief Mighty Bear.

'So . . . so you take the money, there ain't no way yo're gonna git it back to yore folks on the reservation,' declared Lattegan.

'No?' said Little Elk.

'Hell, no! If 'n' you've deserted that reservation, the Army's gonna be out in force lookin' for you. You'll be taken for sure.'

Spotted Tail smiled coldly.

'That is our problem,' he said.

He did not tell the outlaw that he and his companions proposed to continue on their journey north and wait several months till the hue and cry died down. Then, sometime during the course of the following winter, they aimed to sneak back across the border and make their way southwards to Fort Raeburn. A surreptitious visit to the tepee of Chief Mighty Bear would leave him with sufficient funds to provide for his people for some time to come. Lattegan's loot would help alleviate the deprivation suffered as a consequence of the paucity of US Government supplies and the dishonesty of Indian agents like the late Rex Curtis.

'OK, so let's do a li'l hoss-tradin' here,' growled Lattegan. 'Whaddya say we split it fifty-fifty?'

Spotted Tail smiled and shook his head.

'Sixty-forty?'

Again Spotted Tail smiled and shook his head.

'Wa'al, you come up with somethin',' said Lattegan.

'We shall take all of it.'

'Hell, no! You cain't . . .'

'We can do as we wish.'

Lattegan swallowed hard. He knew the Indian was right. There was no chance that he could out-shoot all three of them. If he tried, he would die for certain.

'Aw, come on, fellers! This ain't fair!' he protested, causing Belle to grin suddenly, for these were almost the exact words she had spoken to him.

'Dismount,' snapped Spotted Tail, ignoring the outlaw's protest.

'But . . .'

'Dismount. You too, white woman.'

Lattegan lowered the gun he had been pointing at Belle and slipped it back into its holster. Then he and the blonde slowly climbed down out of their saddles.

'Now what?' he rasped.

'Step away from your horses.'

Reluctantly, both did as they were bid, where-upon Wolf That Speaks and Little Elk rode forward, grabbed the reins of the two horses and led them off a little way.

'Look, let's at least talk. I reckon . . .' began Lattegan, but again Spotted Tail cut him short.

'Throw down your guns.'

'Aw, shucks, surely we. . . !'

'Do it. And do it slowly. Very slowly.'

Lattegan glared at the Indian. He was sorely tempted to go for his gun, but all three Indians' revolvers were out and aimed at him. His chances of surviving a shoot-out were, as he had already assessed, pretty slim. He swore roundly and gently lifted the Colt Peacemaker out of its holster. A glance at Spotted Tail informed him that the brave was keyed up and ready to shoot at the slightest provocation. He lowered his arm and dropped the revolver on to the ground. Then he proceeded to do the same with the gun stuck in his belt.

'Satisfied?' he snarled.

'Kick the guns away from your feet,' replied Spotted Tail.

The outlaw scowled, but did as he was instructed, whereupon Wolf That Speaks quickly dismounted, retrieved the outlaw's revolvers and then promptly remounted.

'You . . . you jest gonna leave us?' enquired Lattegan.

'We are,' said Spotted Tail.

He turned his horse's head and set off northwards, closely followed by his two companions, each of whom led one of the two horses carrying Lattegan's loot. Behind them, Lucky Larry Lattegan jumped up and down in rage and swore fit to bust.

Presently, when he had calmed down a little, Belle asked, 'So, what in tarnation do we do now?'

'I don't know 'bout you, Belle, but I'm gonna head for Providence Flats.'

129

'On foot? Ain't that some fifty or so miles from here?'

'Yup.'

'You'll never make it, Larry.'

'No?'

'Hell, no! There must be half the State of Wyomin' out lookin' for you by now.'

'Mebbe.'

Belle shrugged her slender shoulders.

'Wa'al, I guess I'll walk a ways with you,' she said. 'I don't fancy bein' out here on my own in this goddam wilderness.'

'Please yoreself, Belle.'

Lattegan set off at a fair pace. He realized that, as Belle had just pointed out, news of his escape would have been circulated throughout the State of Wyoming, and there would be others, besides Sheriff Jim Blake and his posse, searching for him. Therefore, the sooner he covered the fifty-odd miles between the Lion's Head and Providence Flats the better. There he would be safe, for Providence Flats was a notorious hell-hole, a town beyond the law. Indeed, a whole posse of US marshals would be needed to prise him out of there. And even that might not be enough. Once he was safely within the limits of Providence Flats, he could relax and plan what to do next.

Belle stumbled along in his wake. The prospect of tramping five miles would have been daunting enough. The idea of having to cover fifty or more on foot filled her with despair. She prayed that she might spot some settlement or other along the way, where she could stop off.

They dropped down from the Lion's Head and then made their way through the foothills of the Medicine Bow range towards the distant plain. An hour passed and they had almost reached the plain when, round a bend in the trail ahead of them, two horsemen appeared. Lattegan immediately halted and, as soon as Belle caught up with him, grabbed hold of her by the arm.

'Hey, Larry, yo're hurtin' me!' she squawked, as his fingers dug into her soft white flesh.

'Shuddup!' he snarled.

The two riders cantered up and reined in their horses. Lattegan eyed them coldly. He recognized US Marshal Matt Gruber, but not the big man at his side. Both men had drawn their revolvers and were aiming them directly at the outlaw. The marshal transferred his gaze to Belle Nightingale.

'Wa'al, wa'al,' he murmured, 'if it ain't Mrs Lattegan! We were told Lattegan had ridden off with some kid, an' all the time it was you.'

'She ain't Mrs Lattegan,' rasped the outlaw. 'She's jest a goddam whore named Belle Nightingale.'

'I ain't no whore! I . . .' Belle protested.

'Leave it, Belle,' interjected Jack Stone. 'We ain't interested.'

'You . . . you know her, Jack?' exclaimed Gruber.

'Yeah. From way back,' confessed the Kentuckian.

'Yet you said nothin'! You let me b'lieve she was Mrs Lattegan!'

'Sorry, Matt. I never figured she'd spring the sonofabitch.'

'Then, what in hell did yuh think she was doin' in Cougar Creek?'

'Tryin' to git Lattegan to divulge whereabouts he'd hidden his loot. If 'n' she did, wa'al, I didn't reckon it was none of my business.'

'But that's what I was tryin' to git him to do!' cried Gruber.

'You had no chance.'

'Mebbe not. Yet . . .'

'Wa'al, I considered Belle might as well have it, rather than it remain buried in the mountains, doin' nobody no good.'

'Which raises the question: is it still buried hereabouts?' Gruber frowned, and directed a puzzled gaze towards the two runaways. 'Another question springs to mind. What are you two doin' walkin'? An' where are yore goddam hosses?'

Lattegan laughed mirthlessly and replied, 'Guess yo're outa luck, Marshal. The loot's gone.'

'Gone?'

'Yeah. We were bushwhacked by a trio of stinkin Injuns, who stole our hosses an' made off with the money I'd buried.'

'Holy cow!' exclaimed Stone. 'Don't that beat all?'

'It sure does,' growled Gruber.

'So, mebbe you oughta git goin' after them redskins?' suggested Lattegan.

Gruber shook his head.

'I don't think so. I figure takin' you in is much more important than chasin' them pesky Injuns. They could be headed anywheres.'

'The leader claimed they were gonna hand over the loot to their tribe back on the reservation.'

'What reservation?' demanded Gruber.

'Dunno.'

'You reckon they recently absconded from this reservation?'

'Yup.'

'Wa'al, can you say what kinda Injun they were: Sioux, Pawnee, Arapaho or. . . ?'

'They all look alike to me. Cain't tell one Injun from another.'

Gruber turned to Belle.

'An' what about you, ma'am?' he asked.

'Me neither,' confessed the blonde.

'Goddammit!' Gruber scowled. 'If 'n' I don't even know which reservation they deserted . . .' he muttered.

133

'You could find out, Marshal,' said Lattegan.

'Guess I could, but that can wait. First I'm gonna take you back to Cougar Creek.'

'Oh, no!'

'What's to stop me?'

'Jest this.' Lattegan stooped and swiftly slid out the double-edged knife from the top of his right boot. Pulling Belle hard against his chest, he drew the blade across the blonde's throat. 'You want me to slit her throat?' he rasped.

'No!' she cried.

'Wa'al, Marshal?'

'Mebbe I don't give a damn,' retorted Gruber. 'After all, she's only a goddam whore.'

'Hey, wait a minute!' interjected Stone. 'Belle ain't no angel, but she don't deserve to die. Not like this.'

'So, what am I s'posed to do, Jack?' enquired the lawman.

'Listen to what Lattegan's got to say.'

'I know what he's got to say. It's his life for Belle's. Right, Lattegan?'

'You got it, Marshal,' replied the outlaw.

'Wa'al, what are yuh gonna do?' asked Stone.

Matt Gruber reflected for a few moments.

'OK, Lattegan,' he said finally. 'You can head on out. I won't try to stop you.'

Lattegan laughed.

'You figure I'm gonna walk, Marshal?' he sneered.

'Wa'al. . . .'

'I need a hoss. Yore hoss.'

'Oh, no!'

'Oh, yes! Otherwise. . . .'

Gruber watched as Lattegan pressed the blade harder against Belle's soft white flesh. One quick movement and he would slit her from ear to ear.

'Give him yore hoss! Please!' pleaded the blonde.

'I also want a gun an' some cash,' stated Lattegan.

'Give him the gun!' she cried. 'I . . . I'll give him the cash. There . . . there's a few dollars in the back pocket of my pants,' she informed her captor.

Lattegan grinned, released his hold of Belle's arm and felt in her pocket for the money. He withdrew a thin wad of dollar bills and slipped them into his jacket pocket. Then he again grasped the blonde's arm in a vicelike grip. Meantime, the blade held tight against her throat had been sufficient to deter her from attempting to escape while Lattegan fumbled for her money.

'OK,' he said, 'now it's yore move, Marshal.'

'I ain't gonna give you no gun; that's for sure,' said Gruber.

'Marshal. . . !' began Belle, but Stone interrupted her.

'Matt's right. He cain't give that murderin' bastard a gun. Yo're gonna have to settle for jest

135

the hoss,' he remarked to the outlaw.

'Now, hang on!' exclaimed Gruber.

'You owe me a favour, Matt,' said Stone.

'So, you saved my life an' I'm grateful. But, hell. . . !'

'It's Belle's life that's at stake here.'

'Mebbe.'

'Certainly. Give the sonofabitch yore hoss an' let him go. We'll catch up with him before too long, I promise you.'

'You cain't be sure 'bout that.'

'But you can be sure, if 'n' I don't git yore hoss, I'll slit the bitch's throat,' rasped Lattegan.

'Wa'al, Matt?' said Stone.

The marshal scowled. He had really no choice. He had to let Lattegan go.

'OK,' he growled. 'Take my hoss.'

He slowly dismounted, pulling the Winchester from his saddle-boot as he did so. Then, he offered the reins to the outlaw.

'Leave 'em danglin',' said Lattegan. 'Then you an' yore pardner mosey on out.'

'Out where?'

'You'd best head on up towards the mountains. At least as far as that there ridge. Figure it's outa range should you or yore pal decide to take a shot at me.'

'Now would we do a thing like that?' asked the Kentuckian, his voice loaded with sarcasm.

'You might,' grinned Lattegan. He turned to the lawman. 'So, git walkin', Marshal.'

'It's OK, Matt, you needn't walk. Climb up behind me,' said Stone.

Gruber thankfully clambered up behind the Kentuckian and Stone urged the gelding forward. The pair cantered up through the foothills, following the trail down which Lattegan and the blonde had recently descended. Presently they reached the ridge Lattegan had pointed out to them. It was a little over a mile from the spot where Lattegan stood, still clutching hold of Belle.

Gruber dismounted and lifted the Winchester to his shoulder. He took aim, then, with a curse, slowly lowered the gun.

'The bastard's way outa range!' he cried.

'Sure he is,' agreed Stone. 'Hell, you wouldn't hit him from here, even s'posin' you had a long-barrelled Sharps rifle!'

'No, I guess not.'

They gazed down to where the outlaw still maintained his iron grip on the blonde.

Belle winced and turned her head to see Stone and Gruber high up on the ridge.

'You gonna let me go now?' she gasped.

Lattegan laughed, a harsh, mirthless laugh.

'Nope.'

'But, Larry, they've done as you asked an'. . . .'

'I don't forgive none too easily, Belle.'

137

'Forgive what?'

'You.'

'Me?'

'Yeah; for desertin' me for a goddam piano-player!'

'Aw, shucks, Larry!'

'Sorry, Belle, but you shoulda stuck with me.'

'You . . . you said earlier you was gonna kill me to prevent me from tellin' anyone where you was headed. But that wasn't the main reason. You planned all along to kill me, didn't you, Larry?'

'That's right,' said Lattegan. Grinning wolfishly, he pressed home the knife and, with its razor-sharp blade, slit the blonde's slender throat from ear to ear. Belle's mouth opened, but no sound came forth. Instead, she spewed out a stream of blood and, as Lattegan relinquished his grip, collapsed in a heap on to the dusty trail. Her eyes stared sightlessly ahead and she lay quite still. Belle Nightingale had sung her last song.

High up on the ridge, Jack Stone and Matt Gruber watched horror-stricken as the murder was committed. Neither had expected such a terrible outcome.

'An' to think I let the sonofabitch go!' exclaimed Gruber.

'Yeah.'

'At yore instigation!' the marshal remarked accusingly.

'Yeah.'

'Holy cow, Jack! Is that all you can say?'

Stone observed the outlaw gallop off towards the distant plain. His face was grim and his eyes as hard as flint. Feelings of cold fury and overwhelming sadness competed within the Kentuckian's breast. He had difficulty speaking.

When, eventually, he did, Stone spoke quietly, yet firmly.

'I'm gonna make sure that evil bastard swings for this,' he said.

'An' jest how d'yuh propose doin' that, considerin' we only got one hoss between us? You gonna abandon me out here an' give chase?' enquired Gruber.

'Nope.'

'Wa'al, he'll be long gone 'fore we git back to civilization an' I can git me another hoss.'

'True.'

'So, unless you know where the sonofabitch is headed for ...' Gruber paused and eyed the Kentuckian speculatively. 'Do you know, Jack?' he demanded.

'I can guess.'

'An' s'pose you've guessed wrong?'

'Then I reckon I'll catch up with him a li'l later than I'd hoped. But, believe me, Matt, I *will* catch up with him,' declared Stone.

'An' for now?'

'We go see to Belle.'

'Belle's dead, Jack.'

'I know.'

Stone urged the gelding forward and they returned at a canter, down through the foothills to the spot where they had confronted the outlaw. Both men dismounted and crouched down beside the prostrate body of Belle Nightingale. Gently, Stone turned her over on to her back.

'Goddammit, Belle, you deserved better than this!' muttered the Kentuckian.

'So, whaddya aim doin', Jack?' said Gruber.

'Whaddya mean?'

'I mean, are you proposin' to bury her out here?'

'Hell, no, Matt! Belle's entitled to a decent Christian burial, an' she's gonna git one.'

'Wa'al, there ain't room for three of us on yore hoss,' remarked Gruber.

'So, you an' me'll take it in turns to walk.'

'All the way back to Cougar Creek?' expostulated the marshal.

'Yup.'

The grim look on the Kentuckian's visage warned Matt Gruber that he'd best not argue.

'OK,' he growled. 'Let's git goin'.'

TEN

It was on the evening of 23 June when Jack Stone and Matt Gruber eventually reached Cougar Creek. They headed straight for the funeral parlour, where Stone made arrangements with the mortician for Belle's funeral, to be held early on the following morning. Then, having left Belle's body in the mortician's care, they crossed the street to the law-office.

Sheriff Jim Blake and his posse had returned to Cougar Creek only a few hours before Stone and the marshal. Having tended to his horse and taken a much-needed bath, the sheriff had repaired to the law-office, where he, his deputy and the mayor were closeted in earnest discussion. All three looked up as Jack Stone and Matt Gruber entered.

'I take it you lost the sonofabitch's trail, too?' remarked Jim Blake.

'Nope,' said Stone.

'We caught up with him in the foothills of the Medicine Bow range,' added Gruber.

'Then, where . . . where is he?' demanded Hiram G. Culpepper.

'We had to let him go,' said Stone.

'You did what?' exclaimed the mayor.

'We had no choice,' said the Kentuckian, and he went on to explain the circumstances under which they had permitted Lucky Larry Lattegan to escape.

When Stone had finished, Culpepper fixed him with an angry stare and cried, 'You let Lattegan go for the sake of the whore who masterminded his escape?'

'Yup.'

'But he killed her anyway?'

'Yup.'

'Wa'al, that jest about beats all!'

'We didn't know he was gonna kill her anyway,' growled Gruber.

'No? Wa'al, I'm surprised that you, a US marshal, should have made such a monumental misjudgement,' said Culpepper pompously.

'Like Jack, I felt that we had no choice other than to let him go,' replied Gruber.

'So, where does that leave us?' enquired Sheriff Jim Blake. 'Accordin' to yore story, Lucky Larry Lattegan is once again free as a bird, while the loot that he'd buried in the mountains is in the hands of a trio of renegade Injuns. Is that the situation?'

'It is,' said Gruber.

'Then, who d'yuh go after? Lattegan or the Injuns?'

'I dunno which Injuns to go after,' confessed Gruber.

'I think I can help you there, Marshal,' interjected Deputy Tom Jeffers.

'Oh, yeah?' said Gruber.

'Yeah. We gotta report that, a few days back, three Arapahos broke outa a reservation some miles south of here. Surely that's too much of a coincidence for them not to be the same Injuns who bushwhacked Lattegan an' stole his loot?'

'Guess so,' said Gruber.

'An' Lattegan told you that the Injuns claimed they was gonna hand over the loot to their tribe back on the reservation?' said Blake.

'He could've been lyin', or they could've been lyin',' replied Gruber.

'That's right,' said Stone. 'They'd be crazy to head back to the reservation, if 'n' they wanta stay free. Hell, the Army's gonna be out in force lookin' for 'em, partickerly in an' around that territory!'

'So, whaddya plan doin', Marshal? Go lookin' for Lattegan, or set out after the Arapahos?' asked Blake.

'I ain't goin' after no Arapahos,' said Gruber. 'If they are headin' back towards their reservation, the Army'll pick 'em up for sure. An' if they ain't, wa'al, they could be headin' almost anywheres.'

'Lattegan could also be headin' almost anywheres,' remarked Culpepper.

'Jack doesn't think so,' said Gruber.

'No?' enquired Blake.

'No,' said the Kentuckian. 'I figure there's one place more likely than any other he'll make for.'

'An' whereabouts is that?' demanded Culpepper.

'Providence Flats,' said Stone.

'Of course! It's only about a day's ride from here, an' roughly the same distance from the mountains,' said Blake. The sheriff frowned. He knew the reputation of that notorious hell-hole.

'You'll never prise him outa there,' he commented.

'Wa'al, it's the obvious place for him to hole up,' growled Stone.

'Yeah. He'll be safe from the law an' can mebbe recruit a new gang,' mused Gruber.

'Are you sayin' the murderin' sonofabitch cain't be touched?' expostulated Hiram G. Culpepper.

'If the marshal rides into Providence Flats, he's a dead man,' stated Jim Blake.

'I can try an' see . . .' began Gruber.

'No, Matt. Even if you hide yore badge, the chance of someone recognizin' you is pretty

144

darned high,' said Stone.

'It's a chance I've gotta take,' retorted Gruber.

'That's right. It's his duty,' stated the mayor piously.

'Then we'll go together,' said Stone. 'I wanta see that bastard hang even more'n you do.'

'OK. When do we set out?'

'Tomorrow mornin'. Immediately after we've attended Belle's funeral.'

'I ain't sure the good folks of Cougar Creek are gonna want her buried in our town cemetery,' said Culpepper. 'I mean to say, she's not only a goddam whore, but also the brains behind Lattegan's escape.'

'She's paid the price,' rasped Stone. 'An' she's gonna have a decent Christian burial,' he added firmly.

Hiram G. Culpepper gulped. The look in the Kentuckian's eye forbade any argument. Stone was not, he decided, someone he wanted to cross.

'What . . . what do you say, Sheriff?' he stammered.

'I guess I go along with Mr . . . er. . . ?'

'Stone. Jack Stone.'

'I guess I'll go along with you, Mr Stone,' said Jim Blake. 'Whatever she's done, it's the Lord who'll judge her now.'

'Oh, OK, then! S'posin' the Reverend Hargreaves don't object,' said the mayor grudgingly.

'The reverend won't object,' replied Blake. He turned to Stone. 'I'll go tell him what's happened. You got any special time you want him to conduct the funeral service?'

'Wa'al, me an' the marshal will wanta set out as soon as possible tomorrow mornin',' said the Kentuckian.

'Then I'll arrange the funeral for nine o' clock. That'll give the reverend time to have his breakfast first.'

'Thanks, Sheriff.' Stone glanced at the marshal. 'That suit you, Matt?' he asked.

'Yup,' said Gruber.

And so, despite Hiram G. Culpepper's misgivings, the matter was settled.

At half past nine on the following morning, Matt Gruber and the Kentuckian rode out of Cougar Creek. Belle Nightingale had been laid to rest. The funeral service conducted by the Reverend Hargreaves had been brief, yet performed in a decent, solemn manner, and Jack Stone was satisfied. Apart from the minister, the only people to attend had been Stone, Gruber, Sheriff Jim Blake, the mortician and the gravedigger. Mayor Culpepper had not put in an appearance.

As they rode beyond the town limits, Gruber turned to Stone and said, 'So, we're headin' for

Providence Flats, but what have you in mind to do
when we git there?'

'Whaddya mean?' asked Stone.

'Wa'al, when the sheriff said he reckoned I'd be
a dead man if 'n' I rode into that hell-hole, you
agreed with him.'

'That's right, Matt.'

'So?'

'So, I ride in. Alone.'

'But you were a law-officer once. There's every
chance that you, too, could be recognized.'

'It's unlikely. I ain't worn a badge in years.'

'Even so . . .'

'I want that murderin' bastard real bad. It's a
chance I've jest gotta take.'

'I s'pose, Jack.'

'Don't worry, Matt, Lattegan's gonna swing for
what he did.'

'I sure hope so. But it could prove tricky prizin'
him outa Providence Flats.'

'Yeah, I know.'

'You have a plan?'

'Sort of. Depends whereabouts in Providence
Flats I locate him. I'll have to play it by ear.'

'An' what am I s'posed to be doin' while yo're
playin' it by ear?'

'There's a ridge close by the trail, half a mile
outa town. I want you there, ready an' waitin', in
case I need yuh.'

'You figure you could be pursued?'

'It's possible. If 'n' Lattegan's made a few friends.'

'OK. We'll do it yore way.'

Matt Gruber reckoned that he had little or no choice other than to accept the Kentuckian's rather sketchy scheme. To insist on riding into town himself would be, he felt, plain crazy. Sheriff Jim Blake was right. Somebody there was almost certain to recognize him.

And so, their plans laid, the two men rode on in silence.

They proceeded at a fairly leisurely pace, for they had a long way to go and did not want to tire their horses unduly. Besides they assumed Lucky Larry Lattegan would not be leaving the safety of Providence Flats for some little time to come.

Their journey was an uneventful one and they reached the low ridge overlooking Providence Flats early the following morning. The trail descended from this ridge directly into the town. Stone reined in his gelding, Gruber doing like-wise.

'So that's Providence Flats, huh?' said the marshal.

'You never been here before?' enquired Stone.

'Nope.'

'It consists almost entirely of saloons, bordellos an' lodgin'-houses. A perfect place for desperate

148

men, with a price on their heads, to hide out, safe from any fear of capture.'

'An' you reckon that's where Lucky Larry Lattegan has made for?'

'I do, Matt. That's where I'd 've headed if I'd been in his shoes.' The Kentuckian smiled grimly. 'Reckon I'll mosey on down there an' see if I'm right.'

'An' what do I do meantime?'

'You hide yoreself amongst that tumble of boulders over there an' keep yore eyes peeled. If 'n' I have to leave town in a hurry, you may need to use yore Winchester to pick off my pursuers.'

'You sure you don't want me to ride into town with yuh?'

'No, Matt. We already discussed this. You stay here till I return.'

'An' jest how long do I wait?'

'How's that?'

'I mean, Jack, I might need to ride in an' rescue you.'

'You don't ride in under any circumstances. I hope to be in an' out pretty darned quick, but, if 'n' I ain't, it could be I ain't comin' out.'

'So, what do I do then?'

'Yo're the US marshal. Guess you'll have to decide for yoreself.'

Again the Kentuckian smiled grimly, then he urged the gelding forward and set off down the winding trail towards the town. Behind him, Matt Gruber slowly dismounted and led his horse into the tumble of boulders that perched on the edge of the ridge. From there he could look down into the town and yet remain unobserved from either the trail or the town. He pulled the Winchester from the saddle-boot and settled down to wait.

Jack Stone, meanwhile, cantered across the town limits and into Providence Flats. He reined in the gelding in front of the Golden Garter, the largest and most popular saloon in town. He hitched the horse to the rail outside the saloon, mounted the short flight of wooden steps to the stoop and pushed through the batwing doors into the huge bar-room-cum-gaming hall.

At that hour in the morning the Golden Garter was devoid of any customers. The solid mahogany bar-counter was empty of glasses and the four bartenders who served behind it were still abed, as were the sporting women and the croupiers who provided for the customers' other needs. Only the proprietor, Frank Cassidy, was in evidence. A slim, swarthy-looking fellow, neatly attired in a black city-style suit, sparkling white shirt, black bootlace tie, dark-green brocade vest and highly polished shoes, he sat at one of the gaming-tables quietly sipping coffee and smoking a large Havana cigar. He glanced up as the Kentuckian entered. There was something vaguely familiar about the stranger, but Cassidy could not, at that moment, recall exactly when and where he had seen the man.*

'Howdy. You jest rode in?' he drawled.

'Yup,' said Stone, pulling up a chair and joining the saloonkeeper at the gaming-table.

'Can I git you somethin'? A coffee mebbe or. . . ?'

'Thanks. A coffee'd be fine.'

Cassidy rose and went and fetched another cup. Then he poured the Kentuckian some coffee from the pot that stood before him on the table. When he had replenished his own cup, he asked:

'You plannin' on stayin' a while in Providence Flats?'

'Nope.'

'Jest passin' through?'

'I guess.'

'On the run, are yuh?' Cassidy smiled wryly. 'Most folks who stop over in Providence Flats are wanted by the law,' he remarked.

'Yeah. Wa'al, I ain't exactly on the run,' said Stone.

'No?'

'No. I have me a li'l enterprise in mind, an' I'm lookin' to recruit some fellers to ride along.'

'What kinda enterprise, if 'n' yuh don't mind me askin'?' said Cassidy.

* See 'The Marshal From Hell'.

'Not at all. There's a bank I have in mind. I figure it's ripe for the takin'. 'Deed, I've checked it out pretty darned thoroughly.'

'An' whereabouts is this bank?'

'I think I'll keep that information to myself. It ain't that I don't trust you, Mr ... er. . . ?'

'Cassidy. Frank Cassidy. I own this here establishment.'

'I figured as much, Mr Cassidy. Wa'al, like I said, it ain't that I don't trust you. It's jest that there ain't no call for you to know.'

'That's fine by me. I quite understand.' Cassidy paused and then asked, 'You gonna tell me yore monicker?'

'Smith. Jack Smith,' replied the Kentuckian.

Both men grinned. Cassidy knew Stone was lying and Stone knew that Cassidy knew he was lying.

'Wa'al, Mr Smith,' said the saloonkeeper, 'you got anyone partickler in mind, or are yuh jest gonna ask around?'

'I have one partickler feller in mind.'

'Oh, yeah?'

'Yeah. Lucky Larry Lattegan. I heard he broke outa jail a few days back.'

'An' you figure he made for Providence Flats?'

'That's what I'd 've done if I'd been him.'

Frank Cassidy smiled, drew on his cigar and blew out a thin stream of smoke. He eyed the

Kentuckian curiously. He still couldn't recall exactly when and where he had seen this tough-looking stranger before. But he decided not to try. 'Mr Smith' struck him as someone it would be unwise to cross.

That he was either a peace officer or a bounty hunter Cassidy had little doubt. Normally, he would have taken steps to ensure that such a man did not leave Providence Flats alive. However, so far Lattegan had not spent one red cent in the Golden Garter, and Cassidy doubted that he was likely to do so in the future. The outlaw was staying at Martha Gurney's, the cheapest rooming-house in town. That indicated that he was practically stony-broke. Therefore, Cassidy determined to let events take their course. If the grim-faced stranger aimed to bring Lattegan in, then he certainly wasn't going to stand in his way.

'Lattegan don't usually take orders from nobody,' he commented. 'He runs his own gang.'

'Only they're all dead or in jail,' remarked Stone.

'True.'

'So, what's he gonna do? Refuse my offer an' stay here till he runs outa money?'

'He could mebbe recruit a new gang?' suggested Cassidy.

'Who'd ride with him? They call him Lucky, but he ain't lived up to that nickname lately.'

'He did escape from jail.'

'At a cost. One of his confederates shot dead an' the other wounded an' taken.'

'You seem to know one helluva lot about his jail-break!'

'I was there in Cougar Creek when Lattegan broke free.'

'Ah!'

'So, Mr Cassidy, did I guess right? Is he here in Providence Flats?'

Cassidy sipped his coffee. He mulled over the Kentuckian's question for some moments. Stone had picked the correct man, for Cassidy liked to keep abreast of all the comings and goings in Providence Flats.

'I guess there ain't no harm in me tellin' you,' he said finally.

'None,' replied Stone.

'He's got a room at Martha Gurney's,' said Cassidy.

'Martha Gurney's?'

'A roomin'-house.'

'I guessed that much. Whereabouts is it situated?'

"Tween Mexican Joe's eatin'-house an' Molly Rainey's bordello, there's three roomin'-houses. Martha Gurney's is the middle one of the three.'

'OK. Which way do I head when I step outside?'

'You turn left. Same side of Main Street as the

Golden Garter.'

'Thanks, Mr Cassidy.'

'A pleasure, Mr Smith.'

Stone finished his coffee and rose. The saloon-keeper remained seated and watched the big Kentuckian cross the bar-room and step out through the batwing doors. He poured himself a third cup of coffee and lit a second cigar. Grinning slyly, he reckoned Lucky Larry Lattegan was in for a nasty surprise.

Outside, Stone remounted the gelding and trotted slowly down Main Street. There were few people about. In Providence Flats its citizens habitually stayed up late and rose late in consequence.

Martha Gurney's rooming-house was a white frame-house with the paint peeling badly, the picket fence in a state of collapse and a mass of weeds proliferating between it and the front door.

Stone dismounted and made his way through the weeds to the door. He banged on it twice and waited.

Moments later, he was confronted by a short, tubby woman, with unevenly cropped, spiky, ginger hair and a decided squint, who was attired in a grubby apron over a faded gingham dress.

'Martha Gurney?' enquired Stone.

'Who's askin'?' snapped the woman.

'I am,' retorted the Kentuckian.

Martha Gurney stared belligerently at the big man. Then her gaze softened slightly, as she noted the look in his ice-cold blue eyes.

'I'm Martha Gurney,' she muttered.

'Good! I have been told you've got a lodger, name of Lattegan.'

'Mebbe I have an' mebbe I ain't,' she replied.

'Does this git me a straight answer?' said Stone, producing a ten-dollar bill and waving it in front of the woman's eyes.

'Make it twenty,' she said avariciously.

'For twenty I need more'n jest a yes or no,' remarked Stone.

'Whaddya need?'

'I need you to take me up to Lattegan's room an' call him out.'

'I didn't say he was here.'

'Wa'al, is he?'

'I git the twenty?'

Stone handed her the money, which she hastily folded and slipped into the bodice of her dress.

'Wa'al. . . ?' said Stone.

'He's here,' she confirmed.

'Then take me to his room.'

'I don't want no trouble. No shootin' or . . .'

'There won't be no trouble if 'n' you do as I tell yuh. Jest call him out. OK?'

Martha Gurney scowled, but nevertheless nodded her head.

'OK,' she said.

She led the way along a dingy hallway and upstairs to the next floor. She halted outside the second bedroom on her left and tapped upon the door.

'Who is it?' came a voice from within.

'It's me, Martha Gurney. Can I speak to yuh for a minute, Mr Lattegan?'

There was a short pause before they heard the sound of someone crossing the room. Martha Gurney promptly stood aside and, as the door was pulled open, Jack Stone stepped in through the doorway and thrust the muzzle of his Frontier Model Colt into the face of the occupant.

'Jesus Christ!' exclaimed Lucky Larry Lattegan.

'One false move an' yo're dead!' snarled Stone.

'Hey, let's not be too hasty!'

'Shuddup an' turn round.'

'But. . .'

'No buts. You murdered Belle in cold blood, an' for no good reason. Wa'al, yo're gonna swing for that, b'lieve me.' Stone's voice was bitter as he reiterated, 'Turn round!'

This time, Lattegan did as he was bid, and immediately Stone reversed the revolver and brought the butt crashing down upon the back of the outlaw's skull. Lattegan pitched forward on to the bedroom floor and lay quite still.

'Darn it, you've gone an' killed him!' cried Martha Gurney.

'No; he'll live,' replied Stone.

The Kentuckian hefted the outlaw up off the floor and across his shoulder. Then he proceeded to carry him downstairs and out through the weeds to where the gelding stood patiently waiting.

Watched by Martha Gurney from the doorway of her rooming-house, Stone fetched a length of whipcord from one of his saddle-bags and tied Lattegan's wrists together. The other end of the cord he attached to the saddle's pommel. This done, Stone climbed into the saddle, turned the gelding's head and set off back along Main Street, dragging the unconscious outlaw behind him.

By the time Stone reached the ridge where Matt Gruber lay hidden, a battered, bruised and bloodied Larry Lattegan had recovered his senses and was on his feet, desperately trying to keep pace with the gelding.

'You got him, Jack!' exclaimed Gruber delightedly.

'Yup,' said Stone. 'An' this time there'll be no mistake. The murderin' bastard'll swing.'

'If he lives that long,' said Gruber, glancing at the perspiring, panting outlaw.

'Aw, he'll live, Matt! I ain't aimin' to kill him, jest give him a kinda rough ride.'

'A kinda rough ride!' cried Lattegan. 'I ain't

ridin'; I'm runnin'! You reckon to make me run all the way back to Cougar Creek, yo're crazy!'

'Then I'm crazy,' said Stone equably. 'Either you run or I drag you. I don't give a damn which.'

And so it was. Lucky Larry Lattegan either ran, stumbled or was dragged all the way back to Cougar Creek. He was indeed more dead than alive when, shortly before noon on 26 June they finally rode into town and came to a halt in front of the law office.

Sheriff Jim Blake promptly took charge of the outlaw and placed him in the cell next to that occupied by Mad Dog Mel. Doc Chalmers was sent for to patch him up, and Deputy Tom Jeffers was detailed to stand guard over him. The sheriff was taking no chances this time.

Since the hangman had not yet left town, the hanging was arranged for eleven o' clock the following morning. Jim Blake was anxious that there should be no unnecessary delay, but wanted Lattegan to have recovered sufficiently to be able to mount the scaffold unaided.

'So, Jack,' said Matt Gruber, when he and the Kentuckian had adjourned to the Prairie Dog Saloon for a few well-earned beers, 'guess tomorrow we'll be goin' our separate ways.'

'Yeah,' said Stone. 'Me to do that spot of huntin' I'd planned an' you, I s'pose, headin' back to the US marshals' office in Laramie?'

'Yup.' Gruber smiled wryly. 'You know, Jack, I don't usually attend hangin's. Not 'less I'm forced. But, after what Lattegan did to Belle, I reckon I'm gonna enjoy this one.'

'Me, too,' said Stone.

They weren't the only ones. The entire population of Cougar Creek turned out for the hanging. Well to the fore were Hiram G. Culpepper and the rest of the town council. Further back stood Sheriff Jim Blake and his deputy, and the US marshal and the Kentuckian, while Mad Dog Mel watched through the barred window of his cell.

On that bright, sunny June morning, six days after his fortieth birthday, Larry Lattegan's legendary luck finally ran out and he was hanged by the neck until he was dead.